The Cannelloni Corpse

A ROMANO'S FAMILY RESTAURANT COZY MYSTERY
BOOK 1

ROSIE A. POINT

The Cannelloni Corpse
A Romano's Family Restaurant Cozy Mystery Book 1

Copyright © 2023 by Rosie A. Point.

www.rosiepointbooks.com

All Rights Reserved. This publication or parts thereof may not be reproduced in any form, stored, distributed, or transmitted in any form—electronic, mechanical, photocopy, recording or otherwise—except in the case of brief quotations for review purposes.

This is a work of fiction. Any resemblance to actual persons alive or deceased, places, or events is coincidental.

Cover by DLR Cover Designs
www.dlrcoverdesigns.com

❋ Created with Vellum

You're invited!

Hi there, reader!

I'd like to formally invite you to join my awesome community of readers. We love to chat about cozy mysteries, cooking, and pets.

It's super fun because I get to share chapters from yet-to-be-released books, fun recipes, pictures, and do giveaways with the people who enjoy my stories the most.

So whether you're a new reader or you've been enjoying my stories for a while, you can catch up with other like-minded readers, and get lots of cool content by visiting my website at *www.rosiepointbooks.com* and signing up for my mailing list.

YOU'RE INVITED!

Or simply search for me on *www.bookbub.com* and follow me there.

I look forward to getting to know you better.

Let's get into the story!

Yours,
Rosie

One

The auditorium in Lake Basil High School brought back memories I would prefer to forget. There was the time that Brittany Brown had pulled my shirt up in front of the entire school—that had been a real hoot. Or the night of the school debate, when I'd mixed up the topics and started arguing the point of the opposing team and had been laughed off the stage.

It was funny how I was almost forty, but those moments were ingrained in my brain, along with the chants of "Pizzaface Romano". I had always felt unworthy of popularity and happiness in this place.

"Gina?"

I blinked, looking away from the main stage, its velvet green curtains drawn to hide the performers, and turned toward Matilda.

My friend, well into her forties, with streaks of gray in her dark hair and wide blue eyes, looked up at me with concern. "You were somewhere else. Are you OK?"

"Yeah," I said. "Just this place brings back a lot of memories. Not great ones."

"Well, that's over now," Matilda said, and looped her arm through mine. She was my best friend, the owner of the little bakery and tea spot opposite my restaurant, and it was strange to see her without her cat, Jumbo. He was her near-constant companion.

"True," I said.

"We're here to have a good time, and that's exactly what we're going to do. How often do we get to see an actual ballet performance in this town?" Matilda grinned happily.

"Try never." Because while Lake Basil was a popular tourist attraction during the summer months, it was the lake and the restaurants that got the most attention. We certainly didn't have a movie theater or even a theater for artistic performances like the ballet in this town.

Matilda and I stood at the back of the auditorium, waiting patiently for Jacob, my boyfriend, and Aunt Sofia and Uncle Rocco, who were my adoptive parents, to join us.

Aunt Sof had spotted the popcorn stand and insisted on buying for us. Jacob had gone with her to help, and

Uncle Rocco had found one of his old friends, Tony, and become embroiled in an argument about basketball. Tony was a Lakers fan—perish the thought.

A soft chime rang through the auditorium, signaling for attendees to get to their seats before the show started.

I couldn't wait to see how this would turn out, especially with the crunching of popcorn in the background and the occasional expletive from one of the locals. You could take the New Yorker to the ballet, and... that was about it. Nothing else would change when it came to how Lake Basilites saw the world—popcorn, basketball, pizza, and swearing included.

"There you are!" Aunt Sofia cried, hurrying over with an enormous bucket of popcorn. "What are you waiting for, girls? Let's find our seats." She patted her dark, frizzy hair—pulled back into a bun for tonight—and cast a look back up the aisle. "Now, where's Rocky gotten off to? I swear, I can't take my eyes off him for a second."

Jacob appeared in the crowd, juggling three more buckets of popcorn, and looking stressed. My boyfriend, who was the chef at my restaurant, was the epitome of tall, dark, and handsome—and harried at the moment.

"How much popcorn do we need?" I asked. "Jacob's about to collapse under the weight of it all."

"Aw, don't be silly, honey," Aunt Sofia said, watching with eager eyes as I took a bucket of popcorn from Jacob to help. "You chose a strong man to be your husband... Oops! I mean, boyfriend."

My cheeks grew hot. "Aunt Sofia!"

"What? I didn't mean it. But, I mean, look at the two of you." She reached up and pinched Jacob's cheek like he was a toddler, then did the same to me. "You're a match made in heaven. Oh! That reminds me, I've got to get a picture of all of us together. This is going to be a night to remember."

I didn't let my irritation show, nor did I look over at Jacob.

We were a year into our relationship, and things were going at the perfect pace for me. Slowly. I didn't want to repeat past mistakes. Even though Jacob was so good, he was almost too good to be true. *Or too good for me.*

"Rocky!" Aunt Sofia waved my uncle over.

A genuine smile parted my lips as my uncle, gray hair and all—he refused to color it like Aunt Sofia did—strode over to us. He was getting on in the years, but he was far healthier than he'd been when I'd first arrived in Lake Basil.

"All right, all right, I'm here," Uncle Rocco said. "Darn, Ned, crying about the Lakers losing against the Nuggets. I told him, I said, I told him that—"

"That's enough about basketball." Aunt Sofia placed a

kiss on his cheek. "We're here to watch the ballet, remember?"

"Excuse me!" A woman shoved past us. "Can you get out of the aisle?" She was a willowy, blonde creature, who was mostly legs, and she gave us a dirty look as she passed. Lake Basilites were blunt, sure, but they were never *rude*, and I didn't recognize her from around town.

Regardless, we filtered to our seats in a hurry. I sat between Jacob and Matilda, so I could whisper to either of them during the evening.

Jacob placed his hand on my forearm and stroked it gently.

I didn't withdraw, but I tensed a little. "Sorry about what my aunt said."

"Didn't make me uncomfortable," he whispered, with a stomach-turning wink.

Stomach-turning because it made me so nervous, I could barely think straight. My last fiancé had ruined my life. And Jacob was just so lovely and—

I have more important things to think about. Like relaunching the restaurant.

I had started upgrades to Romano's Pizza Parlor last year, and it had slowly developed into more than that. People didn't just want pizza, they wanted to spend time with their families, just as I did, and what better way to do that than to rebrand and relaunch?

Music started, played by the orchestra seated off to one side of the auditorium, and the velvet green curtains rolled back, revealing three beautiful dancers on the stage. They wore pointe shoes, and the central ballerina wore a white tutu that sparkled under the lights.

Wonder took hold of me instantly. The dancers moved across the stage, leaping and spinning, their movements so effortless it looked like they floated rather than danced.

The music reached a crescendo, dipped into a lull and—

"Boo! This sucks! You suck." The shout came from a few rows in front of ours.

"What the heck?" Uncle Rocco leaned forward in his seat. "Who was that?"

"You suck! The Little Bear Ballet Company sucks! Boo." The lady continued heckling the dancers.

The principal ballerina, the one in the white tutu, actually stopped dancing and raised a hand to peer out into the darkened auditorium.

"Hey, shut up!" A man shouted from further behind us.

"Yeah." Uncle Rocco shook his fist.

But the lady wouldn't be deterred. She rose out of her seat and continued shouting at the top of her lungs. It was the same leggy blonde who'd pushed past us in the aisle.

"The Little Bear Ballet Company is a fraud. Worst dancing ever. You deserve to die!"

"Wow. What on earth?"

A group of ushers hurried down the aisle toward the woman. The orchestra had gone silent on the command of the conductor, and most of the ballerinas had run off the stage to wait for the disturbance to stop. Except for the principal ballerina. She glared, her skinny arms folded across her chest, and her dark eyes sparkling with malice.

The heckler was dragged out of her seat while we watched. "Let go of me! Let go! Get your hands off of me." But her protests went unheard. She was carried bodily out of the hall, just as the orchestra struck up another song, masking the sound of the doors slamming shut behind her.

Two

The following afternoon...

Tomorrow would be our first test-run before the big launch, and I was pretty darn nervous if I said so myself. I'd consulted for plenty of restaurants in my time, but there was a difference between being outside a business and identifying issues and improvements, and being the one running it.

I had to stay on my toes, and that included preparing everything for tomorrow's soft launch.

"All right, everyone," I said. "Gather round."

The servers, some of whom were newly recruited, and the kitchen staff—Jacob had found a competent sous chef and two other chefs to work the line in the kitchen—took their seats throughout the revamped restaurant.

Romano's Family Restaurant, now serving pasta, antipasti, and pizzas, was gorgeous inside and out. Gone was the vinyl, and the faded menus stuck to the back wall. The interior was rough brick and hardwood floor. The tables were covered in white tablecloths, with lanterns and neat place settings, and there were countless pictures of Uncle Rocco, Aunt Sofia, and me on the walls. Me when I had been that geeky teenage girl or even younger. My first memories had taken place in Romano's and now, this place was mine to run.

Emotion built inside me, threatening to clog my throat. I swallowed and forced a bright smile.

"I'm so glad to have you all on my team," I said. "Thank you for working toward this day with me."

Violet, my sweet server who had been with us for about a year now, twirled a strand of glossy hair around one finger and let it bounce free, smiling at me in anticipation.

Jacob and the other chefs stood to one side, arms folded or leaning casually.

There was an air of community in the restaurant that I'd always wanted but had never quite dreamed could be true.

"Tomorrow," I said, "is our soft launch, as you all know. We're going to be hosting a small party of 12 diners from the Little Bear Ballet Company."

Violet gave an excited squeal and clapped her hands. The guy next to her, Charles, rolled his eyes heavenward at her theatrics. "What's the big deal?" he murmured.

"It's a big deal, Charles," I said, "because these are our first customers and because they're probably going to be a little on the fussy side. Most of them are ballerinas, so they're going to have dietary requirements, and we're going to do our best to make sure that those requirements are satisfied. Capeesh?"

"I got you," Charles replied, dipping his head.

"The soft launch is important because we'll test out how our kitchen runs under pressure and how the front of house operates. Violet and Charles will be tending the table," I said, gesturing to the large round dining table we'd set up for the occasion in the center of the room. "And I'll be managing the bar and aiding you with anything you need that you can't fulfill by yourself. Seriously, if there are any problems, just report them to me, and I'll help you get it figured out."

Everyone nodded except for Jacob.

"That includes the chefs. Any issues? Report to me," I said.

"Outside of actually cooking the food, I assume," Jacob replied, and gave me another of those nerve-inducing winks.

"Of course." My reply was a little on the curt side, and

Jacob's smile disappeared. "So," I continued, "that's it. We're good to go unless you guys have questions. Chefs need to be here at eleven in the morning, servers here a half an hour before opening at 05:00 p.m.."

"I can't wait!" Violet clapped her hands. "This is going to be so cool. Up close with real ballet girls."

"You wildin'," Charles said. "It's not like you're gonna get to talk to them or anything. You're just gonna serve them their vegan water or whatever."

I pressed my lips together to keep from laughing at Charles' assessment. He probably wasn't that far off.

"All right, everybody," I said. "Thanks for coming in today. I appreciate you helping me get everything ready to go. And I'll see you tomorrow. If it all goes smoothly, we'll open the day after. So... there's that." Another bout of nerves came, this one unrelated to handsome chef winks.

The staff slowly filtered out, chatting amongst themselves, Violet walking with a bounce in her step. Jacob stayed behind, and I gave him a quick smile before walking over to the hostess station and removing my handbag from underneath the dark wood countertop. I was keenly aware of Jacob's gaze fixed on the back of my neck.

"What's up?" I asked, turning toward him.

"Any reason you're being snappy with me?"

I squared my shoulders. "I didn't intend to snap like that. I'm sorry about it," I said, then took a breath.

"But?"

"But we're in a precarious situation here. We work together, and we're dating. I lo-like being around you a lot, and we're good, but we need some separation between our personal and professional life," I said. "Like, the whole winking at me thing in front of everyone. I don't want any of the staff to think I'm playing favorites because we're dating."

Jacob didn't say anything right away. He tucked his hands into the pockets of his jeans and tilted his head, expression was pensive. "I get it," he said. "No problem."

"Look, I don't want things to be awkward. It's just how it has to be at work."

"Sure," he said. "It's not like everybody knows that we're dating or anything."

I stiffened. "Jacob," I said, "I didn't mean we should keep it a secret or stop seeing each other, just that we should stop the PDAs at work."

"If a wink is a public display of affection, then…"

"It is," I said.

Jacob released a low breath. "Sorry," he said. "I know you're coming from a good place. I guess I've gotten a vibe from you lately that you're… going through something? And I can't help wondering if it's got something to do with us."

"No," I said, "nothing like that. It's just work." And

that was a lie. A white lie. I had my concerns about our relationship, but it wasn't anything fatal. It was more about me and my feelings. Nothing had *actually* changed.

"OK, cool." Jacob smiled easily, twisting my heart around his little finger. "Do you want to go grab some dinner?"

"Actually, I have a dinner date with Matilda and Jumbo."

"Oh sure," Jacob said. "Have fun. I'll text you later."

"That sounds great, Jacob." I gave him a quick hug goodbye, then scooted out of the restaurant and across the road toward my friend's bakery, my heart pitter-pattering away at my deception.

Three

Matilda's bakery had become a second home to me since my return to Lake Basil. I stepped through the front door and was immediately embraced by the smells of fresh-baked chocolate chip cookies and the usual warmth that had nothing to do with the fact that it was summer. It was the atmosphere here.

The bakery was pink, white, and teal, with sparkling tiles, glass counters stacked with treats, a tea spot off to one side, and a chaise lounge in front of the window where Jumbo, Matilda's cat, lay sunning himself.

Jumbo was large and white and utterly adorable. He loved the attention from all the friendly Lake Basilites who stopped by Matilda's bakery for a bite to eat and a "spot of tea" as she liked to say when channeling her British heritage.

I went over to Jumbo and sat down on the chaise lounge beside him, unbothered by the white fur that would surely stick to the seat of my pants. I'd trade a white furry butt for a few minutes of Jumbo's happy purrs any day.

The bakery was relatively empty since it was late afternoon and almost closing time, so I waited it out, smiling and waving at Matilda behind the counter.

"Be with you in a sec," Matilda called.

Fifteen minutes later, the last of the customers were gone, and Matilda turned the cute little sign in her glass front door from OPEN to CLOSED.

"Gina," she said. "You made it."

"It was a short walk across the street." I grinned back at her.

Matilda brushed her hands off on her cute, pink apron and gave Jumbo a scritchy-scratch behind the ears. He purred and yawned, stretching out his white furry paws. "I'm surprised you wanted to hang out this evening," she said. "I thought for sure you'd be busy with Jacob."

"Busy?"

"It's a Saturday," she said. "That's usually classed as a date night for young people."

"Young people? You're like five years older than me."

"Five years in cat years maybe," Matilda replied, then raised an eyebrow. "And I sense you're deflecting. Why?"

"No reason."

"Other than?"

"Oh, I don't know," I said. "I've been thinking about things lately, you know, with the big relaunch coming and all of that."

"Tell me about it while we head upstairs." Matilda lived above the bakery with Jumbo, in her comfy apartment that overlooked the street below and the pizzeria, coincidentally. I followed her upstairs, mulling over what I wanted to say rather than actually saying it.

Jumbo gave an imperious meow and ran ahead of us, his fluffy white tail and swishing through the air.

Matilda opened the door for him, clicking her tongue at his impatience to get to his food bowl, and I followed her inside and went over to the floral sofa in front of her TV. I plopped down, kicked off my shoes, and tucked my feet underneath me.

"So?" Matilda prompted from in front of her fridge. She rooted around inside and then brought me a bottle of water.

I accepted it gratefully, the coolness against my palm a reminder of just how hot summer could get in Lake Basil. Thankfully, we hadn't gotten into the thick of it yet.

"So," I sighed, "I wanted to get away from everything for the evening."

"You mean you wanted to get away from Jacob."

Matilda took a seat across from me, her phone in hand. "I would say let's get pizza but..."

I snorted. "I'm fine with whatever you want. And yeah, I wanted to get away from Jacob, as horrible as that sounds. I've been having some confusing thoughts about him and our relationship lately."

"Thoughts such as?"

"Such as—" Was I really going to put this into words? I trusted Matilda, but it was still difficult to air out my thoughts about this topic. It was a weakness. I'd come out of a ruined relationship, and the thought that it might happen again terrified me. "Such as maybe we're moving too fast or that he... He just seems too good to be true."

Matilda wriggled her nose from side-to-side but didn't say anything.

"I keep waiting for something bad to happen. I don't know why that is," I said, scratching my forehead.

"Maybe because things have been going so well lately," Matilda replied. "Think about it. Your dreams are coming true. You've got a handsome boyfriend, your uncle and aunt are happy, you have friends, and your business is succeeding. It could be that a part of you doesn't want to believe it's true because of everything you went through with Larry."

"The cursed ex," I murmured.

"Exactly."

She might've been right. Or it could have been nerves about the launch of the restaurant. Whatever it was, I'd have to hope it would pass with time.

"Let me ask you this," Matilda said, after a silence filled with Jumbo's happy crunching at his food bowl, "how far would you go to help a friend in need?"

"To the ends of the earth," I said instantly.

"And you consider Jacob a friend."

"Well, that's true but different. Kind of."

"How far would you go for the person you love?" Matilda asked.

I chewed on my bottom lip because I didn't have an answer. Which wasn't like me. I prided myself on having an answer for most things and making snap decisions. I'd been trained to do that after years of working in a corporate setting. The early bird got the worm, and I was the earliest bird.

Matilda gave me a smile. "Chinese?"

"Sounds great."

She got up and walked through her tiny, cozy apartment, chatting amiably on the phone to Wei, who always took our order at Potsticker Palace, leaving me to contemplate what we'd discussed.

I went over to the window, anxiously twisting the top of my water bottle, and peered down at the restaurant.

The new sign was up, glowing red, green and white, against the bricks above the new awning.

Romano's Family Restaurant.

Family. Family was more than just the people you were related to. Family was friends, it was caring, it was community, and I had wanted to portray that in every inch of my business and life.

"Admiring my new setup?" Matilda asked beside me.

I nearly jumped out of my skin. "Sheesh." I massaged my chest. "Be sneakier next time."

"Sorry." Matilda grinned, then gestured to the black bulb on her windowsill. Not a bulb, but a camera on a tiny stand watching the street below.

"Wow," I said. "What's this for?"

"Security purposes," Matilda said. "And I like to live vicariously through other people as I watch them continue about their daily lives."

I laughed.

"Honestly, I've been thinking about getting one for a while, ever since that stuff happened at your pizzeria last year."

The aforementioned stuff had included dead bodies and murder investigations.

"I figure it's a good idea, you know? Good way to keep track of things in case anything goes wrong out in the street," Matilda said. "And if Jumbo ever gets lost, I have a way of tracking him that doesn't just involve the GPS tag on his collar."

I couldn't help but laugh again as I looped my arm through my friend's and we walked back to the sofa together. Matilda had also been through it before she'd come to Lake Basil, so I didn't blame her for her precautions. I appreciated them.

"Let's hope you'll never need it," I said.

Four

The following evening...

THE SOFT LAUNCH HAD GONE OFF WITHOUT A hitch so far. Violet and Charles tended to the center table of dancers, artists, and friends of the Little Bear Ballet Company with smiles on their faces. The entrees had come streaming out of the kitchen, hot and perfectly seasoned, and I hadn't had one hiccup or complaint.

I stood behind the bar in the restaurant, watching my servers work the table with pride.

My anxiety from yesterday was gone—maybe it had just been the restaurant's launch that had been bugging me—and I watched the guests with intrigue.

I'd had the pleasure of being introduced to each of

them when they'd entered the restaurant. And there were familiar faces among them.

The principal ballerina, Giselle, with her glossy black hair in a tight bun atop her head, sat closest to my side of the bar. She was as elegant off the stage as she was on it, and she was seated beside her brother, Jordan, who was the artistic broody type.

To Giselle's left was the Ballet Master, who was in charge of the dancers—Cole Bernardo. He ate his entrée with neat, perfectly portioned bites, and didn't talk much to the other guests at the table.

I understood why Matilda liked people watching so much. It was fascinating to take in their interactions and make personal assumptions and connections. Or I was reading into everything because I so desperately wanted them to love the restaurant as much as I did.

The guests seemed happy, after all. They'd been chatting and switching chairs with one another throughout the evening so they could talk to different people. It felt like a real party.

My server, Violet, stopped next to the table to check on everything, bending close to Jordan and Giselle, a smile parting her lips. She nodded, then turned and came toward me at the bar.

"What's wrong? What's the problem?" I asked, my anxiety rising.

"Nothing serious, Gina," Violet said with a bright smile. "Just that one of the customers wants to talk to you about the tiramisu."

"The tiramisu?"

"Uh-huh."

But they hadn't touched the tiramisu. They weren't even on the main course yet. *Easy. Relax.*

What was wrong with me? I was never this tense. I'd dealt with plenty of crotchety or even downright angry customers in the past.

I inhaled through my nose, then rounded the bar and went to the table.

Jordan, the brother of the principal ballerina, gave me a dark-eyed look as I approached and waved me over. "Ah, Gina, right?"

"That's correct," I said.

"Jordan." He placed a hand on his chest.

"I remember, sir," I said. "What can I help you with? My server mentioned that you have a question about the tiramisu?"

"That's correct," he said. "I wanted to make sure that you got my previous message about the tiramisu. I left it with a woman at reception yesterday when we made the booking?"

"Ah, yes, that's right. That was me," I said with a smile. "You wanted the cream in the tiramisu to be vegan. Is that correct?"

"Yes. It's very important that my sister only has vegan food," Jordan said, pressing a hand to his sister's forearm.

Giselle looked up momentarily before continuing her conversation with Cole, the Ballet Master. Those two talked on a more intimate level, not that it was any of my business.

"Yes, that's not a problem," I said.

"You're sure about that?" Jordan asked. "Because you are serving cannelloni with beef in it. And we wouldn't want the meat to transfer over if that makes sense? Like, you don't cook the vegan food in pans that were used for the meat, do you?"

"No, we don't, sir," I said. "Absolutely not. We have strict rules about dietary restrictions and requirements, and I assure you we've taken your sister's needs into account."

Across the table, a gorgeous young woman with fiery red hair, Kate, scoffed loudly. The Ballet Master had introduced her as a soloist, not that I knew what that meant.

That got Giselle's attention. She glared across the table at the other woman, and a few of the other guests fell silent, pausing their conversations to watch the tension zipping between the two of them.

"Have you got something to say to me, Kate?" Giselle

asked, in a too-sweet voice. "Because it seems like you've got a lot of opinions to share lately."

"Easy," the Ballet Master said. "We're at dinner, you two. We're not going to ruin the evening because of this."

"I'm not ruining anything," Kate said, her accent smacking of Boston. "What, I can't have an opinion anymore?"

Cole lifted his hands, shaking his head. "Let's just keep things calm this evening. That's all I'm saying."

"Yeah, shut it, Kate." Jordan placed a hand on his sister's forearm again and glared at the redhead across the table.

"Jordan." The Ballet Master snapped out his name. "That's enough. Out of everyone. Just enjoy your evening."

Slowly, the other ballerinas returned to their meals. Kate and Giselle stared at each other, pure hatred radiating across the table, before returning to their conversations.

Jordan finally turned back to me. "Yeah, so anyway. It's all arranged?"

"Absolutely," I said. "I'll double-check on it for you, though."

"Thank you." Jordan gave a relieved smile.

Whatever anger he had toward the woman across the table wasn't carrying across in his attitude toward me. Once again, it wasn't any of my business, but I didn't doubt Matilda would find this entire conversation fascinating.

I left the guests to their entrees and chatter—and hopefully with a helping of peace rather than tension—and peeked into the kitchen.

Jacob was hard at work. He caught my eye and smiled at me, the unhappiness from yesterday already gone and forgotten.

My heart squeezed at the sight of him, passionate and happy as he worked, and I smiled back. "Just checking you're taking all the dietary requirements into account? I don't doubt you, but one of the diners is asking about it."

"Absolutely. You're talking about the principal ballerina, right? Vegan tiramisu for dessert, and meatless cannelloni for mains."

I gave him a thumbs up. "Thanks, Jacob."

"No problem."

I swept back out of the kitchen and to my spot at the bar, watching the guests with renewed interest after the mini-spat I'd witnessed. They finished their entrees and my servers swept in to remove the dishes and ensure that all their drinks were full.

The talk continued, with a few of the guests rotating around the table or heading off to the bathroom. The only person who didn't shift seats was Kate.

Not long after, more plates arrived from the kitchen,

the main meals. Ravioli, cannelloni, pizza, puttanesca pasta, and more. My mouth watered at the smells of tangy tomato, garlic, and cheese that wafted over from the table.

The customers ate their meals, appreciating the flavors and nodding excitedly at each other as they ate. Success. My insides warmed at the—

Giselle rose from the table, clasping at her throat. She made a choking noise and stumbled back a step, staring at her plate in horror.

"Giselle?" Jordan leaped to his feet. "Sis? What's wrong?"

Five

Giselle gasped and shook her head, clutching her throat dramatically. Multiple people rose around the table. Jordan circled to where his sister stood. He foisted the glass into his sister's hands. She drank from the glass, gasping dramatically afterward while everyone in the restaurant stared at her.

"Is everything OK?" I asked, walking over to them.

Giselle took a deep breath. "I-I-I believe there's meat in my cannelloni."

"Seriously? You're freaking out about *that?*" Kate's words whipped across the table, but Giselle ignored her this time.

Relief traveled through me—for one horrible moment, I'd been sure that Giselle was choking—and I removed the dish from the table right away. "I'll check on this for you,"

I said. "I'm so sorry about that." I would've gone all out on the apology, but I wasn't convinced that Giselle was right.

Jacob was great at making food taste... Well, great. Meat or no meat. Could it be that Giselle had made a mistake? I'd been super specific about there *not* being any meat near the vegan food.

"You do that," Jordan said in a low growl.

"I think I'm going to go to the ladies' room," Giselle said, pressing her fingers to her forehead. "I feel faint." And then she left the table.

I headed toward the kitchen, questions forming in my mind. There was *no way* my chefs would mess this up. I'd briefed them thoroughly, they were accomplished cooks, and I'd reminded them about the vegan requirements on the customer's insistence.

Something was off here.

I entered the kitchen through the swinging doors and headed over to the metal counter that separated the line from the area where the servers picked up dishes. "Jacob?"

"Yeah." He swept over, a cloth strung over one shoulder of his chef's whites. "Everything OK?"

"Apparently not. I've got a diner out there claiming that the cannelloni has meat in it."

"The vegan cannelloni?" Jacob's tan brow wrinkled. "Impossible. I check each dish before it leaves the kitchen myself."

"That's what she's saying," I said.

"May I?" He held out a hand.

I gave him the dish, and Jacob inspected it, opening the cannelloni with a knife and fork.

"It's the vegan option," he said, handing it back to me. "One hundred percent the vegan option. She must've been mistaken."

"I'll talk to her."

"Do you need me to come out there?" Jacob asked.

I gave him a pleasant smile. "Nope. All good." I was used to conflict by now—it was better to face this type of thing head on, and I was the owner of the establishment. I wasn't about to let my staff take the brunt of a customer's displeasure, and judging by how Giselle and Jordan had been acting this evening, they were going to fight me on this. Call it a gut feeling.

I returned to the table. Jordan was speaking to Giselle in a hushed tone as I brought the meal back to them.

"Well?" Jordan asked, imperiously. "What does your chef have to say about the mix-up? I assume you're going to pay for all our meals after this. It's so unprofessional. I told you, Giselle. I told you we should have never agreed to come to a new, untested restaurant."

"There's nothing wrong with the restaurant." Cole, the Ballet Master, leaned back in his chair, his lean arms folded over his chest.

"You would say that," Jordan snapped. "You're the one who chose this place. I ought to—"

"I'm sorry to interrupt," I said, "but the cannelloni is vegan. I had the chef check it for you, and it is our vegan option and was prepared as per your specifications."

"Are you calling me a liar?" Giselle fisted her hips and made that look elegant even in her anger.

"Yes," Kate called.

Jordan gave her a withering expression.

"I'm not calling you anything, ma'am," I said calmly. "Our chef is so good at what he does that he makes it easy to mistake the vegetarian and vegan options for the real deal."

"I don't accept that," Giselle said. "I demand a full refund for the meal."

The customer was "always right", but she was so *wrong* it hurt. That didn't matter. The rational business owner part of my brain said I should comp her meal and call it a night. We didn't need critical reviews floating around on social media.

"I can happily replace this meal for you if it's not to your satisfaction," I said. "And I am more than happy to offer you a free dessert for your troubles."

"That would be fine," Giselle said at last. "Unbelievable. I really can't—"

"What's going on?" Jacob walked over to us, drying his hands on his cloth, his eyes sparking with irritation.

Oh no. This is the last thing we need. I put the plate of cannelloni down on the table and squared my shoulders. Jacob coming out of the kitchen would only make things worse rather than better. Why had he bothered? I'd told him I could handle it.

"Is there a problem?" He stopped in front of Giselle, and Jordan sized him up.

"Yes, there's a problem," Jordan said. "You fed my sister meat. You're lucky I don't call the health inspector on this place or go to the papers about your utter negligence. How many times did I have to ask for vegan options? And you failed to deliver. Unbelievable. I—"

"You're wrong," Jacob said, getting straight to the point. I hadn't seen him this angry before. "The meal is vegan. If you think it's not, that's on *your* tastebuds."

"Ex-cah-use me?" Giselle lifted a finger and poked his chest. "You're lucky you have a job with an attitude like that."

"Don't touch me, lady," Jacob said. "I'm telling you the truth. I prepared a vegan meal for you, and if you—"

"Don't you talk to my sister like that!" Jordan roared.

If the others hadn't been watching before, they certainly were now. I took a breath to calm myself, then put a hand on Jacob's shoulder and squeezed. "It's all right, Jacob. I've got this under control."

"I demand," Giselle said, "that this—" She cut off and swallowed, swiping a hand over her head. She blinked and swayed. Was it just me or was she even paler than she'd been when she'd first sat down at the table? "This..."

"Giselle?"

"I demand you fire this man," she whispered, trembling on the spot.

"Look at how much you've upset her!" Jordan grabbed hold of his sister's elbow to steady her. "Giselle, it's all right. You didn't eat much of it. You—"

"I—" Giselle stumbled forward a step, and Jacob backed away from her. I didn't blame him. She looked as if she was about to toss what little cannelloni she'd eaten onto my brand new floor. "I—"

"Ma'am?" I stepped forward. "Are you—?"

A throaty gargle escaped Giselle's pale lips. She keeled over. I put out my arms to catch her. Jacob did as well, but we were both too late. Giselle collapsed onto the wooden floor with a heavy thud. Screams and gasps rose from the table.

Six

"You can't be serious," I murmured. "This can't be happening." I said the words more to myself than anyone nearby.

The ambulance had arrived shortly after my call to 911—I hadn't found Giselle's pulse and she was out cold—and they had carried her out of the restaurant on a stretcher. Her brother had gone with her, his face wan and drawn.

The police were on the scene too, including my old high school acquaintance, Shawn Carter. He'd been a linebacker in high school, and he hadn't lost his broad shoulders or the easy confidence that came with it. He had lost his hair, however, and a lot of his patience.

He was a detective now, and he stood near the table, talking to the guests who sat shell-shocked by tonight's events. The doors were open, allowing in a blast of warm night air from outside that made me sick to the stomach.

I sat on a barstool with Violet on my left and Charles on my right. Neither of them were talking as we waited for whatever would come next. Hopefully, we'd find out later that this was all a symptom of something other than food poisoning.

The fear that our food had made her ill was both valid and terrifying.

"All right, everyone," Detective Carter said, "I'm afraid your evening is over. You're all going to leave. My partner will take your details, and you will have to remain in Lake Basil until further notice."

"What? Why?" That came from Kate, who had risen from her seat, her glittery black clutch in her hands. "Just because Giselle got sick? Ugh, the girl is such a drama queen. Trust me, she'll be fine."

Detective Carter sighed. "I'm afraid that's not the case. Miss Prentice is no longer with us."

All around the table, faces dropped. Kate's eyebrows rose. The guests filed out of the room one by one, giving their details to the police officer waiting at the door. No one could leave until they'd surrendered their information to him.

I watched them, but only because my mind was refusing to catch up with the information he'd given us.

This is not *happening again.*

Not that I'd had a customer die on me before, but a dead body in my restaurant? This wasn't the first time. It felt like a curse.

"Hey," Jacob murmured, grabbing hold of my hand underneath the bar top. He squeezed. "I'm here. It's going to be OK."

I opened my mouth to respond, but Shawn Carter strode up to us, and I thought better of it.

"Gina," he said, nodding. He didn't look at Jacob. "I'm sorry to do this to you, but you're going to have to shut this place down for a while."

"What? That's—"

"What's going on?" Violet whispered. "How did she die?"

"I don't like this," Charles said. "Don't like it one bit. She just kind of fell over. She—"

Shawn gave them a tight smile, then asked them to wait by the kitchen doors. They scooched off their seats and did exactly that, their arms folded.

Tension threaded through me. "Shawn, what's going on? I know you said she passed, but why are you making everyone give you their names? What do you think is going on here, exactly?"

Detective Carter sighed, stroking his broad jaw before running his hand over his bald pate. "Look," he said, "I need your chef here to get the others out of the kitchen. I want them all standing by that wall over there. Nobody touches anything, got it?"

"What the—?" Jacob frowned. "Are you out of your mind? Why would we do that?"

"Because I told you to," Shawn barked it out. His face softened as he turned to me. "Gina, is there a backdoor in your kitchen?"

"Yes," I said.

"Is it unlocked?"

"I haven't unlocked it this evening," Jacob said, his stare burning into the side of Shawn's face. There was so much tension in the air, it threatened to choke me. *Poor choice of words.*

"Good," he said. "Keep it that way. Get the chefs out of the kitchen and wait for further instructions."

Jacob walked off without another word, opening the door to the kitchen and calling to the other chefs in a voice that was gruffer than usual.

"What exactly is going on here, Shawn?" I asked.

"Giselle is dead," he said, "and from what your guests described to me, it sounds like she's been poisoned. I'm waiting for the preliminary report from the medical examiner, but something ain't right."

"Such as?"

"She died after eating cannelloni from your kitchen. Served by your chefs."

This was unconscionable. "Detective, there's nothing in my kitchen that could hurt or harm or… kill a customer. If there was, I wouldn't be in business."

"Something poisoned a woman tonight, Gina," Shawn said softly. "And it had to have come from inside this restaurant. I'm going to need you to talk me through what happened tonight."

"I—" I took a breath, then nodded. "OK." I told him everything I'd witnessed, sparing only the details that I thought were unnecessary.

"Right," Shawn said, taking notes with a pen and pad as he listened to me. As we talked, other cops filtered through the restaurant, carefully cordoning off the table.

"You said that she had a problem with the cannelloni specifically?" Shawn asked. "You sure about that?"

"Yeah," I said. "She thought it wasn't vegan."

"What gave her that impression?" he asked.

"I'm not sure. Just that it tasted like meat or something? She didn't give me any specifics, but she seemed furious about it."

"As angry as your chef when he confronted her about it," Shawn said.

"You can't seriously be suggesting Jacob had anything to do with this. He doesn't even know her. What would the motive be?" This wasn't the first time I'd had to think critically about a dead body or a mystery, and the longer we stood here talking, the clearer my mind became.

"It's not so much about motive, Gina, as it is about who had access to that plate," he said. "Why would she have kicked up a fuss about meat in the food if there wasn't meat in the food?"

"There wasn't. I checked with Jacob."

"Did you taste the cannelloni?" he asked.

"No."

"Where's the plate?"

"On the table over there," I said, pointing it out. "I put it down when Jacob came out of the kitchen to talk to her."

"And that conversation was heated," Shawn said.

"Yes, but that was because she was screaming. I think Jacob just wanted to defend me. He didn't have anything against her," I said.

"And now you're defending Jacob in turn. How sweet."

"Are you being sarcastic, Detective? Shawn, what is—"

"I need to talk to your chefs now," he said. "And I might need to talk to you again, Gina. Don't leave town, all right? I've got your number. I'll call you if I need you to come down to the station."

"I—"

Shawn strode off toward the kitchen doors where the servers and chefs waited. I stared at his back in disbelief. He thought we'd done this.

And he had a point. How on earth had a poison or deadly substance gotten into my kitchen? And how had it wound up in Giselle's cannelloni?

Seven

The following morning...

I wrapped my hands around the cup of coffee, blinking and bleary-eyed in my aunt's kitchen. I had managed a few hours of sleep at the most and they hadn't exactly been restful. I didn't normally dream, but last night had been full of nightmares about Giselle, plates of cannelloni, and Jacob's expression morphing from calm to rage and back again.

"Gina, honey," Aunt Sofia said, as she shuffled into the kitchen wearing her robe, her frizzy hair brushed back into a ponytail. "There you are. You're up early. You want something to eat? I was just about to fix your uncle some breakfast."

"What are you making?" I croaked it out and cleared my throat.

"Waffles. And no, I don't want any help before you ask." She gave me a warm smile to soften the blow. "You look like someone dragged you backward through a bush. Hurry and finish that cup so I can pour you another one."

I shut one eye to better focus on her then sighed. "I assume you heard the news."

Aunt Sofia's eyes gave the game away, but she grabbed the coffee pot without answering and held it aloft. "Looks like we need a refill." My aunt, as kind and blessedly lovely as she was, preferred to avoid hard conversations rather than face them head-on.

"A woman died in my restaurant last night," I said. "If you're keeping score, that's about three people near Romano's, either inside or outside, that have died. Been murdered."

Aunt Sofia's hand trembled at the word. Instead of answering, she tied on her kitchen apron in a business-like fashion and moved over to the sink to pour water for the coffee.

"Three people," I murmured. "Is my business cursed?"

"Don't talk like that, Gina. It's not right."

"Mmm." I bumped my hand onto my forehead. "That poor girl. I mean, sure, she was a little on the melodramatic side, but she didn't deserve that. Nobody deserves to be poisoned."

"Was that what they said it was?" Aunt Sofia broke. Her desire to avoid difficult things often warred with her love of gossip. You could take the woman out of the salon, but eh, the habits stayed, didn't they?

"Shawn seems to think that she was poisoned. And he definitely thinks that one of the chefs had something to do with it."

"Oh, come on, now. One of the chefs?" Aunt Sofia asked. "Why? What's the point?"

"That's what I said. No motive. Doesn't make sense to me, but Shawn's the detective, right?"

"Shawn's a good detective," Aunt Sofia said. "But so are you."

"You fall and bump your head this morning?" I asked.

She swatted me on the head with a kitchen towel. "Don't talk like that. I swear I taught you better. Besides, it's true. You practically solved those murder cases on your own the last time around. Remember?"

"I don't think there's enough whiskey in New York to make me forget that."

"So negative," Aunt Sofia said, and swatted me a second time.

"Ouch."

She pinched my cheek before moving through the

kitchen to pull out bowls and a mixer. My aunt loved caring for me and for my uncle, even though I felt like I was a burden on them by living here. After all the money and time I'd poured into the restaurant revamp, I didn't have money to move into my own place, and my aunt and uncle had been super patient with me about it.

I didn't want to cramp their style too much, especially since it was Uncle Rocco who'd gifted me the restaurant. Of course, I made sure he got money from the restaurant as well, even though he'd insisted I take the place and that was that.

"Shawn has his reasons," Aunt Sofia said suddenly.

"Huh?"

"For doing what he's doing."

"Auntie?"

"You'll see what I mean." Aunt Sofia mixed batter in a teal plastic bowl, turning toward me with a knowing expression on her face. "But I know you wouldn't hurt a fly and neither would any of your employees. You've always been an excellent judge of character, Gina."

I opened my mouth to offer a rebuttal, but the shrill of the front door buzzer stopped me. "I'll get it."

I got up, brushing my messy hair behind my ears, and stumped down the hall, trying not to let my bad mood show too much. I passed the living room, where Uncle Rocco sat with his feet up, watching the morning news.

"What's he talking about?" he shouted, shaking the remote control at the TV over some imagined or real slight.

I smiled to myself and opened the front door, adjusting my white cotton robe as I did.

Detective Carter stood on the concrete front step, his green eyes bright, and his shirt perfectly pressed. He wore a lanyard bearing his ID, and he held his phone in one hand, the other resting on his belt.

"Shawn?"

"Gina," he said, with a smile that made him much more approachable. "Rough night?"

"I—" I touched a hand to my hair. "Thanks."

"Sorry." Shawn grimaced. "I meant that last night wasn't good for nobody. Mind if I ask you a couple of questions?"

"Sure. Why not?" I was going to spend the morning worrying about what Shawn had found anyway. And this way, I could pressure him to tell me when we could get back into the restaurant, clean up, and prepare for the launch.

It sounded darn selfish to think of it that way—a woman had died—but I also had people relying on me. Entire families who relied on the restaurant to pay them and to feed their loved ones.

Shawn came into the cramped hall and squeezed past

me, his cologne leathery and warm and not all that unpleasant. He gave me an awkward smile before striding toward the living room. He stopped in the doorway. "Morning, Mr. Romano," he said.

"Shawn? What are you doing here?" Uncle Rocco squeaked upright in his reclining chair.

"Just here to talk to Gina."

"Ohhhh. I see." Uncle Rocco winked.

What was *that* about? Maybe Aunt Sofia hadn't spilled the beans about what had happened at the restaurant last night.

"We can talk in the kitchen," I said. "Aunt Sofia's making waffles if you want some."

"That's generous of you." He followed me down the hall and into the kitchen.

"Shawn!" Sofia patted her hair. "Goodness, what are you doing here this early? My, you're looking like your father more and more each day."

"Thanks," he said, and gave her a quick hug. He sat down at the table, and I filled up a cup of coffee for him before taking my seat.

"So," I said. "What's the news?"

I could feel my aunt listening in, not that it would strain her much to do so.

"I'm afraid it's poisoning," Shawn said. "And that it came from somewhere in your restaurant. We're still not sure how it got into the food, but it looks like murder, Gina. I'm sorry, but Romano's is going to have to stay closed for the foreseeable future."

"You've got to be kidding me," I said. "I understand this is serious, but I don't see how this is possible. None of my chefs would—"

"Jacob, you mean," Shawn interjected.

"Huh?"

"Jacob was the only chef who handled Giselle's food," he said. "And apart from your server, Violet, who served it, you were the only other person who touched that plate."

I didn't have a reply.

Aunt Sofia sniffed as she brought out her waffle iron and set it on the counter.

"You understand that this is serious, Gina," Shawn said. "I'm going to need to talk to you down at the station at some point. I wanted to warn you about what's been happening out of courtesy."

"Courtesy," I managed.

"That's right." Shawn rose from the table, his coffee mug untouched. "Stay safe. I'll be in touch." And then he strolled out of the kitchen as if he hadn't given me the worst news imaginable.

Eight

I would not let this murder case endanger my boyfriend, my staff, or my restaurant. I didn't care what Shawn thought. I knew that none of my staff were capable of murder and there had to be a logical explanation for why this had happened that didn't include them killing a customer.

Giselle definitely had enemies.

I had to throw my mind back to the previous evening and the tension at that table to realize that. Someone had wanted her dead, and I had my suspicions about who that might be.

After a delicious breakfast, I thanked my aunt, said goodbye and headed out of the front door, purse in hand and determination in my step.

If Shawn believed Jacob had done this, I had to find out who'd killed Giselle before he did something drastic. I got the impression that Shawn didn't like Jacob, and while I respected the detective for his professionalism, I wasn't sure how far that would extend when it came to my boyfriend.

My heels clicked on the sidewalk as I headed for my Honda Accord, parked out front. It was a short drive over to Violet's apartment on the other side of town. Violet roomed with her sister and her brother-in-law, and when I hit the buzzer on the front of the building, the sounds of chaos greeted me.

Pots clanged through the speaker, followed by a shout. "Violet?" I called. "Hello?"

"Hello? Who's there?"

"It's Gina. Is this a bad time?" I shouted it, attracting a strange look from a guy passing by in the street.

"No." More banging and shouts. "Come on up." The buzzer went off, and I headed upstairs to her floor. I knocked once, wincing at the continuous racket from within.

The door opened a second later and Violet peeked out. "Gina," she said, with a bright smile. "Come on in. Don't mind the mess. Grace and Carlo are having a bake-off."

I entered the small apartment and ducked as a spatula

whipped past my head and hit the flatscreen TV on the wall. The place was cramped, but full of noise and light. The open-plan kitchen was where the action was taking place.

Violet's sister, tiny but a firecracker, stood beside the counter, hurriedly plopping flour into the bowl. Carlo, her lanky boyfriend, had his hair tied back and crouched in front of the cupboard, tossing pots, pans, and utensils over his shoulder as he searched for whatever he was looking for in there.

"Would you keep it down?" Violet called. "I have a guest."

The pair ignored her, so Violet gestured for me to follow her down the hallway and into her bedroom. It was decorated in shades of lavender, true to her name, and she'd pasted several pictures of the roman Colosseum on the wall over the desk.

She flopped down on the edge of her bed, gesturing for me to take a seat. "I got your message about the restaurant being closed by the cops." Violet pulled a face. "That sucks, Gina. I'm sorry."

"It is what it is," I said. "Look, Vi, I'm sorry for bugging you at home, but I had to talk to you about something."

"Sure. What's up?"

"I wanted to ask you about last night. Shawn's saying

that Giselle was poisoned, and that it was somebody in the restaurant who did it. He said that it was only you, me, and Jacob who touched the plate of cannelloni responsible for Giselle's death."

"Yeah," Violet said, interlacing her fingers and squeezing them. "Yeah. He talked to me about that. We had a whole interview down at the station last night after you left. It was real bad."

"Bad?"

"Yeah. He was mad suspicious of me," Violet said. "Even though I didn't do nothing wrong. You know?"

I nodded. "Here's the thing, though," I said, "he's not lying about whatever killed Giselle. He's just trying to figure out who poisoned her meal. And I want to know the truth as well. The sooner we figure out which sicko killed her, the sooner her killer will be brought to justice and we can get back to work."

"Yeah, of course. OK." Violet bobbed her head.

"So, I know that it wasn't you, me, or Jacob. But it had to be somebody," I said. "So, did you see anything suspicious last night?"

"You mean, apart from the way that one redhead girl was hating on Giselle all night?"

"Kate," I said. "I noticed that. Did you happen to see if Kate went anywhere near Giselle's side of the table?"

"No," Violet said. "No, I mean, she didn't leave her

seat like the others. Everybody else was getting up and talking. But the redhead didn't move around at all. I thought it was kind of weird at the time. Like, she didn't want to talk to anybody but the people on her side of the table."

"Did you see anything else notable?"

"Huh." Violet scratched her chin.

The quiet was punctuated by another crash in the kitchen.

"Huh, actually... I noticed that Giselle got up and went to the bathroom at one point. And so did the other guy, that one who was sitting next to her."

"Who? Her brother?"

"No, the other guy. He sat next to her at the beginning of the night, but they all kind of moved around. I don't know, it was confusing."

"Cole? He was wearing a black shirt and slacks. Very neat guy? Sort of skinny."

"That's the one." Violet clicked her fingers. "I didn't think much of it at the time, but when she got up to go to the bathroom, I saw him following her."

"Was this before or after she complained about her food?" I hadn't noticed Cole get up from the table when Giselle had mentioned the meat in her cannelloni and said she felt sick.

"No, it was right before the food came out. They both

got up. Well, she did first, and then he followed her," Violet said. "You don't think he did something to her, do you?"

"I don't know," I replied. "But I'm gonna find out."

Nine

After my chat with Violet, I needed a tea break to think about the information I'd gathered so far. Not much, all in all, but heading down to Dingle's Bakery was a good excuse for hovering around near my restaurant and spying on the cops and what they were up to.

I parked my car out front, then got out and cast a quick glance toward Romano's. The awning, green-and-white striped and flapping gently in the early afternoon breeze, shaded the front door, which stood open. Two crime scene investigators worked inside behind a police line, while another stood out front, gloves and booties removed, on a smoke break. The investigator, a woman, eyed me suspiciously.

I lifted a hand in greeting, which she didn't return.

Somebody's in a good mood. I didn't want to read too

much into what that meant, so I entered the bakery and found it buzzing with activity.

Matilda's hair stood on end as she rushed around, tending to nosy and well-intentioned Lake Basilites who had come to gossip about the murder at my restaurant.

The minute the door clapped closed behind me, the noise in the bakery silenced. Heads turned. Eyes widened.

That's just fabulous.

I smiled around at a few familiar faces—Grace from Cara's Coffee down the street, and Fredrick from the barber shop—before heading over to my favorite spot next to Jumbo's chaise lounge. The kitty was stretched out as per usual, his fluffy white belly on display.

"Hey, Jumbo," I whispered, as the chatter started up again.

Jumbo purred, stretched and clutched his kitty paws to his face. I stroked his belly idly as I waited to be served.

Matilda had one other girl working with her—a sixteen-year-old from Lake Basil High who was on her summer break—and she hustled over to greet me, her cheeks pink.

"Hiya, Gina," she said, whipping a stubby pencil out from the pocket of her apron. "What can I get for you this afternoon?"

"Hi Layla, how are you?"

"Sweating like a mouse in a cat's house," she said, with a shrug.

"Even with the aircon? In that case, I'll take a peach iced tea and a slice of carrot cake please."

"I'll bring that out for—"

A crash shattered the happy hum of talk in the bakery, and a few people cried out at the sudden noise. It had come from the street.

A fancy red sports car smoked outside, its front bumper having collided with the back of the forensics van.

The woman who'd been on break outside Romano's stared, jaw-dropped, her cigarette drooping from between her fingers.

A man emerged from the sports car, his dark-eyed gaze fixed on the damage and a scowl twisting his conventionally attractive face.

I sucked in a breath. *Jordan?*

The brother of the victim stumbled a step onto the sidewalk, clasping either side of his tan face as he stared at the point of contact between his car and the van in horror. Jordan stalked toward the woman on her break, throwing one arm toward the vehicles, his voice rising loud enough to be heard within the bakery.

I jumped off my seat and hurried outside, intrigue and concern driving me onward in equal parts.

"—park in this spot," Jordan shouted. "Are you out of your mind?"

"Sir, I'm going to have to ask you to lower your tone," the woman said.

"Lower my tone? If you hadn't parked in such a stupid place, this would never have happened. I can't believe you—"

"What's going on?" I stopped behind Jordan's car.

Jordan spun toward me, and the woman took that moment to whip her phone out of her pocket and walk off up the street, muttering about calling for assistance.

"You!" Jordan pointed at me. "What are *you* doing here?"

I didn't have to answer this guy's questions. It was a free country. "Are you all right, Mr. Prentice? Do you need medical attention?"

That took the wind out of his sails a little. He clasped his forehead momentarily, running his hand up into his caramel-brown hair and tugging on it. Jordan's eyes were bloodshot, and the front of his shirt was creased badly. The same shirt that he'd worn at dinner last night, notably.

"I—I don't know what happened. I was just driving down the road, and—then—" He blinked and swallowed.

"I think you might have fallen asleep behind the wheel," I said, walking over to him and placing a hand on his arm. "It's all right, Mr. Prentice. I understand that you've been through a lot. Why don't you take a seat while we wait for an ambulance to arrive and check on you?"

"Ambulance?" Jordan swallowed, and tears welled in his eyes. "My sister. The ambulance."

"I know," I said. "But you might have a concussion. Come on, come over here." I guided him to one of the benches that were common on Lake Basil's broad sidewalks. He sat down on it, swallowing and gripping his head again.

"I'll sit with you until they arrive. Just try to breathe evenly and relax as much as possible. Are you feeling dizzy?"

"No," he said. "Just tired. I—Did I crash into that van?"

I nodded. "Did you sleep at all last night?"

"No," he said. "Not after... No." Jordan turned to me. "You were the one—" He shook his head. "No, this is *his* fault. I'll make him pay for this. It's all his fault!"

"Who?"

Jordan blinked rapidly as if he hadn't realized what he'd been saying. "I—The Ballet Master.'

"Cole?"

A hesitation. "Yes. It was him. He's the one who did this to her."

"Your sister? Do you mean you think that Cole Bernardo poisoned your sister?" I asked.

"Yes," he murmured. "Yes." The second affirmation came with a stern tone and an increase in volume. "Yes!" A shout. "He did this to her. He wanted her out of the way because he didn't love her anymore! It was him. He did this to her. He—"

"The police are on their way." The crime scene investigator had returned. "And an ambulance. He all right?"

"Relatively," I said. "There's a lot going on at the moment."

"You're telling me." The woman rolled her eyes toward the front of my restaurant.

I turned back to Jordan to check on him, but he had slumped back against the bench and stared up at the sky. "Why?" he asked. "Why? Why? She was a good person. A kind person. And I—Why?"

He was taking his sister's passing badly, and I didn't blame him. I didn't have any siblings, but if one of my family members passed, I would be inconsolable. I was grateful I hadn't had to go through the grieving process yet. The most I had grieved for was the death of my engagement to a real piece of work.

I patted Jordan's shoulder. "I know, Mr. Prentice. This must be so difficult for you. I'm sorry, but help is on the way, all right? Help is on the way, and you're going to be fine."

"Me? But what about *him*?" he asked, turning a hazy-eyed gaze on me. "What about *him*?"

"We'll have to leave that to the police." It was the most comforting thing I could think to say, but Jordan let out a tiny sob afterward.

In truth, I wouldn't be leaving anything to the police. And what Jordan had told me was enlightening and a new connection between the attendees of the dinner party.

Violet had told me that Cole and the victim, Giselle, had risen from the table at the same time or close to it before the main meals were served. And now, Jordan was convinced that his sister had been killed by Cole because "he didn't love her anymore."

A relationship gone sour?

Ten

That night...

Jacob could've stepped off the cover of a magazine. He had chosen a buttoned shirt for this evening, rolling the sleeves up over his strong, tan forearms, and he had shaved for our date tonight. He gave me an easy smile as he buttered a piece of bread from the basket our server had placed on the table.

It had been a while since we'd had an official date night, and tonight, we had chosen a cute steakhouse that was priced well and popular with local Basilites. Basil and Beef was decorated modestly, with square tables, rustic brown stools and a bar that spanned one wall and held a specials board behind it.

"What are you interested in tonight?" Jacob asked,

perusing the menu idly as he chewed on his bread. "The T-Bone looks delicious."

"Huh. Yeah, maybe." My mind was scattered. The murder, the car accident from earlier and the closure of the restaurant were all bugging me. Not only had I been called into Shawn's office to be questioned about the murder, but I'd found out that Cole and the other members of the Little Bear Ballet Company were staying in a local guesthouse. They couldn't leave town yet, and I'd been considering going over there and asking the man a few questions.

But I had to have a good excuse for doing that. It wasn't like I was a cop and Cole would just reveal his whole life's story when I prompted him. I needed a—

"Gina?" Jacob's fingers brushed over the back of my hand.

I looked up from the spot I'd been staring at on the tablecloth. "Sorry," I said. "I was somewhere else."

"That much is obvious," he said, with another of his enigmatic smiles. "My question is what's got you so deep in thought. The restaurant?"

"Everything, Jacob," I said. "I don't mean to be negative, but I feel like we're sitting on board the Titanic, eating a meal as it sinks. Like in the movie with the musicians? Remember?"

"Sure," he said, but his words were clipped. Jacob was seldom impatient with me, or hadn't been over the past year since we'd started dating, so why now? Was it because of the vibe I'd been giving off?

An awkward quiet drifted between us, and I sighed. "I'm not trying to ruin the evening," I said, sitting back and readjusting the silk blouse I'd chosen for our date. "But this is just—"

The server came over to take our order, and I bit back my frustration and forced a smile. "I'll have what he's having," I said, gesturing to Jacob.

I didn't usually let a man make my decisions for me, regardless of who the man was, but I didn't have the mental energy to figure out what I wanted for dinner tonight. And, for once, I didn't have an appetite. Maybe it was that carrot cake I'd inhaled after I'd seen Jordan to the ambulance. Sugar was good for shock, right?

I didn't even hear what Jacob ordered for us. I took a sip of mellow red wine and swished it around my mouth, trying but failing to enjoy the bouquet.

"Gina?"

"Yeah." I put down my glass. "I was thinking about the restaurant and, you know, the fact that Shawn's been questioning you. And me."

"Yeah," Jacob said. "I was hoping to get away from that for the night."

"That's sweet, Jacob, and I agree with you to a certain extent, but haven't you noticed how everyone in this room is staring at us." I'd been trying to ignore it since we'd entered, but there were several tables who'd been gossiping and glancing over at us since we'd sat down.

"I can't say I care," Jacob replied. "They'll arrest the guilty party soon enough, and then it won't matter what anyone thinks, will it?"

"Optimistic."

"Realistic," Jacob said. "You and I both know we haven't done anything wrong. Besides, We know what killed her, and neither of us have that particular substance in our homes or lives. Unless you've had a sports injury I don't know about."

"Not following you," I said.

"Oh? You haven't heard?" Jacob asked. "I saw it in the newspaper this morning. Headline news."

"I try to avoid the news," I said. "Makes my blood pressure rise. What did they say?"

"Apparently, it was oxycodone."

"That's—"

"An opioid painkiller," he said. "And there was enough of it in her system to knock a horse over."

"Wow. Wow, that's—" I didn't know how to describe it.

That had to mean that someone had had access to that drug, which could only be prescribed, and had specifically put it in the cannelloni dish. But how? There had been only a few moments between when the dishes had arrived at the table and Giselle had started eating. Granted, I hadn't been paying a lot of attention to her actions specifically—how could I have known that she was about to die?

The only time I'd been concerned with her was when she had risen from the table and accused Jacob of giving her meat in the cannelloni. And she'd hurried off to the bathroom saying she was sick.

Had she been poisoned then?

The only other time it could have happened was when the dish had been taken back to the kitchen and Jacob had checked it.

My heart skipped a beat, and I reached out and clutched his hand, swallowing.

"What?" he asked.

"Just thinking about when I brought that dish back to you. If it was poisoned then, which it probably was, if you'd tasted to check it was vegan instead of visually checking..." I squeezed his fingers in mine.

Jacob gave me a soft smile. "Good thing I didn't. Though, your detective friend seems to think that makes me more suspicious."

"Wait, what?"

"Carter? Yeah, he asked me why I didn't taste the dish to check it didn't contain meat," Jacob said, stroking the backs of my fingers before releasing my hand again.

"Apparently, telling him that I had prepared it personally and knew exactly how it had been cooked and what had gone into it wasn't convincing enough. There were only two vegan dishes at that table, anyway." Jacob shrugged. "Apparently, me eating the poisoned dish would've been far better for Carter's investigation and would have ruled me out as a suspect."

"That's kind of backward." And I wasn't a fan of how Jacob had called him my "detective friend."

"That's what I thought," Jacob said. "Now, can we enjoy the rest of our evening without worrying too much about this?"

"Yeah," I said, "of course." I wasn't so much confused about the case anymore as I was determined to figure out what had happened. It was clear that Shawn thought Jacob had something to do with this. I would stop at nothing to make sure I proved him wrong.

Eleven

I kissed Jacob goodbye on the tiny front step of my Aunt and Uncle's house, then watched him cross the equally small garden. He got into his BMW and waved me inside, refusing to leave until I had gone in.

Inside, I kicked off my shoes, flexing my toes and groaning at how cramped they'd been in my fancy high heels. I didn't often get to wear the designer clothes and shoes I'd bought when I'd been working in the City, so it was nice to treat myself once in a while. I peeked out of the front curtain to check Jacob was safely on his way, then turned and nearly knocked my aunt over.

"Honey!" Aunt Sofia exclaimed, bright-eyed and bushy-haired. "There you are. How was your date?" She grabbed hold of my hands and stroked her fingers over the backs of mine.

My aunt was lovely and affectionate and always had been, but this was a weirdly specific move.

"What are you doing, Auntie?"

"Hmm?" She dropped my hands, a flash of disappointment crossing her face.

"You can't be serious," I said. "You thought Jacob was going to propose?"

Aunt Sofia fluffed her hair and stepped back a pace. "How was your dinner? Are you still hungry? Did you have dessert? I made apple pie while you were gone. Would you like a slice?"

"Don't change the subject," I said, advancing on her. "I know what you're up to, Auntie, and it's not going to work."

"Apple pie is lovely with clotted cream. Not a summer dish, but I didn't want to make another fruit parfait, you know. There's only so much yogurt—" Aunt Sofia was schvitzing.

"Auntie!"

"What's going on out here?" Uncle Rocco padded around the corner, barefoot and looking ready for bed. He had the TV remote in hand. He had a habit of dozing off late at night.

"We were just talking about Auntie's propensity for interfering in my relationships," I said. "Or this one at least."

"Apple pie!" Aunt Sofia squeaked and hurried off in the direction of the kitchen.

I walked down the cramped hall and gave Uncle Rocco a quick kiss on the cheek. "Off to bed?" I asked.

"Now? Nope. Not when Sof is bringing out the apple pie." Uncle Rocco grinned at me then gestured for me to follow him into the living room.

I did, taking a seat on the sofa and folding my tired feet underneath myself. The TV was muted, a basketball game playing in the background, and Uncle Rocco lowered himself into his reclining chair with a sigh.

"How was your night, Gina?"

"It was good," I said. "I mean, we talked a lot about what happened at the restaurant."

"Darn crazy people in this town," Uncle Rocco grumbled. "I heard it was oxycodone that did it."

"Yeah," I said. "And Shawn believes that Jacob might have had something to do with the murder itself. Though how he can think that is beyond me."

"I think I know how." Uncle Rocco didn't have a chance to elaborate.

Aunt Sofia swept into the room carrying a tray with three plates of apple pie, each with a dollop of cream on top. She doled them out then settled into the armchair next to my uncle's.

The clink of dessert forks on china was the only sound for a few moments.

"I heard you talking about Shawn," Aunt Sofia said. "I don't think he would needlessly accuse anyone. Are you sure he thinks it was Jacob?"

"That's what Jacob seems to think," I replied, taking another bite of my pie. It was warm enough to melt the cream a little, and it was deliciously spiced and sweet.

"It doesn't seem likely," Aunt Sofia said, "that Shawn would think that. He has to know that Jacob wouldn't hurt a fly."

"No motive," Uncle Rocco said.

"Exactly." Aunt Sofia lifted her fork with a flourish. "But I heard a rumor from Nancy down at the library today."

"Related to the murder?" I asked.

"Mmm, yeah. She said she heard that Giselle had been arguing with some lady with blonde hair before they went to the restaurant."

"Wait, what? What do you mean?" I set my plate in my lap, considering.

"I'm not explaining it right," Aunt Sofia said, clearing her throat. "Nancy's friends with old Beau at the Lake Basil Guesthouse, and apparently, Beau had to break up an argument between Giselle and some blonde girl out front."

"A blonde girl."

"Yeah. And she wasn't part of the ballet company," Aunt Sofia continued, "because she wasn't staying at the guesthouse with the others."

"That's strange." It didn't make sense to me why someone who wasn't part of the ballet company would have had an issue with Giselle. After all, Giselle and the Little Bear Ballet Company were from out of town. They were just passing through, and they'd done Lake Basil a favor by putting on a show for the locals, potentially because Beau was connected with the town council and had offered them free accommodation.

That being said, Giselle didn't know anyone in Lake Basil. So where had this blonde lady come from?

"Wait, so did Beau recognize this woman?" I asked.

"No. He had no idea who it was, only that they had a heated argument the night before. He didn't say about what, just told Nancy that it was loud enough to disturb his other guests, and he had to go out there and threaten to call the cops if they didn't let up. Apparently, that spooked the blonde girl, who ran off."

"Huh." I ate another piece of pie, turning this new piece of information over in my mind.

"Ah, I've got it," Uncle Rocco said, into the silence. He had a blob of cream on his chin. Aunt Sofia reached over and wiped it off for him.

"Got what?" I asked, checking the basketball game on the screen.

"The blonde girl."

"Oh?"

"Remember when we went to watch the ballet?" he asked, with a twinkle in his eyes. "There was that wretch who started screaming during the performance and had to be escorted out. The rude one."

My eyes widened. "You're a genius, Uncle."

"Don't know about that. Might not even be the girl you're looking for, but you never know. She's not from around here, so that could be the reason Beau didn't recognize her."

And it made sense. That woman would've had a motive for getting rid of Giselle. She'd been furious with the ballet company or the dancers, though the reason for her anger wasn't clear. There was one problem with the theory.

She hadn't been in the restaurant at the time of the murder. And she certainly hadn't had any contact with the food. The back door of the kitchen had been locked, and unless one of my servers or chefs was friends with her, I didn't see how she could be involved.

I hid my disappointment from my aunt and uncle, opting to eat the rest of my apple pie in silence.

Regardless, the blonde woman was a lead I would check out after I ticked off the first task on my list.

Find and talk to Cole Bernardo, the Ballet Master, and Giselle's alleged lover.

Twelve

The following morning...

THE BUMPY ROAD THAT ENCIRCLED LAKE BASIL'S namesake was an eclectic part of the town at this point. The locals complained about it ceaselessly, but nobody ever did anything about it. It had become a part of what it meant to live in Lake Basil, so I gritted my teeth and bore it as my Honda bumped over the dirt road.

I found the Lake Basil Guesthouse in a spot that overlooked the lake itself. It was early, but there were already people out in boats on the lake, fishing or enjoying themselves, happy that summer had finally come.

And the town was happy that tourist season had come along with it.

There was a camp that ran on the far side of the shore,

and kids would soon arrive. I'd gone to Lake Basil Summer Camp as a kid, and it had been a fun experience, full of swimming, camp food, and ghost stories after dark.

My middle school years had been better than high school, that was for sure.

I parked my car further back on the grass, away from the vehicles of guests parked out front—SUVs and coupes, fancier than I'd seen in a long time, and a van bearing the name of the ballet company. I headed past a tire swing hanging from an old oak tree and approached the double story building with its wraparound stoop. The doors were open, despite the early hour, and Beau was seated at the reception desk.

He smiled at me as I walked up the front steps.

Before I had a chance to greet him, Cole Bernardo came down the stairs, walking at a leisurely pace, a newspaper in one hand and his gold-rimmed glasses perched on the tip of his nose.

It was strange to use the word about a man, but he seemed elegant.

I waved to Beau then turned to Cole. "Hi, Mr. Bernardo."

He shifted his glasses off his nose and peered at me. "Hmm. I know you from somewhere. Ah. The restaurant. Is that correct?"

"Yes," I said. "I hoped to catch up with you before you

left the guesthouse for the day."

"Leave? I have nowhere to go," he said. "Besides the lake, I suppose, but I prefer staying indoors during summer. UV rays. Bad for the skin."

"Sure," I said.

"What did you want to talk to *me* about?" He neatly folded the newspaper then dropped it on the reception desk as he passed it on his way toward me.

"Let's step outside," I said. "If you don't mind?"

"That depends on what you want to talk about." He had a warm smile, but it didn't reach his eyes. He wasn't a bad-looking man, just unconventional. Almost androgynous.

We stopped on the stoop a short way from the door, and I clasped the railing with one hand, tucking my purse tight to my side. The morning's heat was soft compared to what the day would bring, but I was glad I'd opted for a sleeveless blouse and cut-off shorts. Mr. Bernardo's stare made sweat gather on the back of my neck.

It was an intense stare that pierced right through me.

He cleared his throat delicately.

"Right," I said, "I wanted to ask you about a woman."

"A woman. You'll have to be more specific than that."

"A blonde woman." I'd prepared my plan over a cup of

coffee this morning. I had to have a reason for questioning Mr. Bernardo, and one that didn't involve a straight up question along the lines of "ay yo, why did you poison your girlfriend?"

"Again, more specifics required."

"Sorry, it's the heat that's melting my brain," I said.

"And this conversation is fast melting my patience."

"Uh, there's this blonde woman who's been bugging people around town. Yesterday, she made a fool of herself in front of my best friend's bakery." White lies abounded. "She's not from around here, and when I started asking questions about her, I heard that she might've had beef with you."

"With me?"

"Or your ballet company," I said. "I'm only asking because I want to report her to the cops for disturbing the peace, and I don't know what her name is."

"Oh." Cole took a deep breath in through his nose. "I think I know who you're talking about."

"You do?"

"Yeah. Emma Silver," he said. "She used to be a part of the Little Bear Ballet Company, actually."

"She did?"

"She was the Ballet Master before me," he sighed. "It's part of the reason I've been having so much trouble with

Kate recently. Emma used to be in charge and she wanted Kate, her cousin, to be the principal ballerina. I stepped in and changed things up. She took umbrage." He scratched his forehead with long, artistic fingers. "Not that any of this matters. It appears she's lost it if she's making an issue around town about things that don't concern her."

"OK, thank you. I'll have to report her to the cops," I said, letting out a breath.

I'd gotten that bit of information at least. Now came the tricky part. "She didn't like Giselle or her brother, did she?"

Cole gave me a quizzical look. "What gave you that idea?"

"I mean, if she wanted Kate as the principal ballerina and then you replaced her with Giselle, it follows that—"

"What has that got to do with her disturbing your best friend's bakery?"

"I was just curious," I said. "Consider me a nosy townsfolk with nothing better to do. You know, I heard that you and Giselle—"

Cole waved a hand. "I have no idea why you think you can talk to me about Giselle."

"I'm just—Well, I'm sorry for your loss, Mr. Bernardo. I know that you must have been close with her. I talked to Jordan about—"

"That's what this is really about, isn't it?" Cole's face

had gone red. "Jordan Prentice. That... That... Hmm. Nope. I am not doing this now." He walked past me, heading for the inn's doors then stopped and turned back, the wooden boards creaking underfoot. "Did he put you up to this? Talking to me? That lout—"

"No," I said. "He didn't put me up to anything. I barely know him. I just wanted to ask about the blonde—"

"Then I have nothing more to say. Nothing." And with that, he stormed back into the inn, leaving me with a case of the cold sweats.

He was a scary man. I didn't know why, but there was something terrifying about how precisely he moved and talked. It was as if every thought had been calculated beforehand. I tugged on the front of my blouse and flapped it back and forth, generating a little wind over the girls.

I swallowed and hurried down the front steps toward my car. I wasn't going to hang around and wait for that guy to come out again. Sure, I was from the City, but that was exactly why I was pressed about this guy. I always got the tingles when there was a dangerous person around, and that was exactly how Cole Bernardo made me feel. Like I had to watch my back, or he'd be the one who stabbed it.

I got into my Honda and started it, ready to peel out

of the driveway. A glance in my rearview mirror stopped me before I slammed the car into reverse.

Kate, the redhead who had despised the victim, strolled around the corner, carrying a brown paper bag of groceries, a smile parting her lips.

Thirteen

I put my car in park and got out as Kate approached, glancing toward the guesthouse to make sure that Cole was inside.

Kate hummed under her breath. Her gaze flickered toward my face and she did a double-take. "Hey, I know you," she said. "You're the restaurant lady, right?"

"Sure, that's one way of putting it." Today, I was the sweaty lady or the lady who had totally panicked when trying to question a suspect. "Kate?"

"Yeah," she said, stopping and shifting her groceries from one arm to the other. "Say, you served us some wicked pasta the other night. Apart from you know, the cannelloni that killed Giselle." She grinned like it was a joke.

"Thanks, I guess?"

"Totally," Kate said. "I was just going to bake some muffins in celebration of—uh, just because it's a nice day."

Random. "Do you have a minute to talk, perhaps?"

"Talk? Sure. What do you wanna talk about?" Kate beckoned for me to follow her over to the tire swing that overlooked the lake. She set her bag of groceries down in the dirt next to the swing, then sat on the tire resting her heels in the dirt and swaying back and forth gently.

"I wanted to ask you a couple of questions about Giselle."

"Oh. Great." She rolled her eyes. "That's *all* anyone wants to talk about lately."

"She did just die, you know," I said.

"Whatever. Trust her to go and get herself poisoned and steal the limelight yet again. I mean, I finally got my part as principal in the ballet back now that she's gone and died, and now all anyone can talk about is how she's dead."

So the muffin-baking was in celebration of her role as the new principal ballerina. "Wow, that's amazing," I said. "Congratulations, Kate."

She flushed, smiling out at the placid waters of the lake. Everything around Lake Basil was green and lush during summer—it was the reason the town and the lake had earned their name. "Well, let's just hope I eventually get to perform once we're allowed to leave this dumb town."

"Because of the investigation?"

"Exactly. The detective doesn't want to let us leave, and he keeps questioning us on rotation, like he's going to squeeze information out of us," she said. "Whatever. It's only a matter of time until they catch the person who did it and then we can forget about Giselle and move on with our lives."

"You *really* didn't like her, huh?"

"Like her? I hated her with a capital friggin' H." Kate kicked up some dirt. It seemed like she wanted to vent to someone. I was more than happy to comply. "She was such an attention-seeker. Like, she couldn't stand it that I was the principal. And then Cole took over, and that was it, right? She just gets chosen to be the principal. Ugh."

"You think that Cole did that because of his relationship with Giselle? They seemed close when they were chatting at the restaurant the other day."

"Uh, no?" I could practically see the question marks in Kate's eyes, like I was ludicrous for suggesting it. "Cole is a fair guy. He does what he thinks is right for the ballet company. Personally, I think it's because her brother sort of co-owns the ballet company."

"Jordan?"

"Yeah," Kate said, checking her nails. "It's nepotism. There's no way Cole would choose Giselle over me. And well, it all ended in my favor anyway. I'm the principal ballerina, and there is literally nothing anyone can do about it." She swiveled the tire swing toward me and skewered me with a stare. "You know, Giselle told me I was too fat?"

"She did?"

"Uh, yeah. So, a couple of months ago I got really sick with a stomach bug," Kate said, "and I obviously didn't eat a lot. So when I got back into class, Giselle acted all like she didn't know I had been sick or whatever. And she asked me if I'd been sick, and when I said yes, she was all like, 'I can tell, you've lost weight.' Like, who says that to another person? She was *so* gross."

"That's mean."

"Right?" Kate flicked her hair over her shoulder. "So, I guess somebody got over her being mean to everyone and killed her at last."

"She was mean to other people? Not just you?"

"I was her main target because, obviously, I was her biggest competition," she said. "But yeah, she was pretty mean to the other ballerinas too. The only person she wasn't rude to was Cole, and that was for obvious reasons."

"Reasons such as—?" I'd heard from Jordan that Cole and Giselle had been dating, but I hadn't had actual confirmation of that from the Ballet Master himself. It would help if I could at least hear it from someone else who had witnessed it.

"I mean, she had to be nice to him? He was in charge," Kate said. "Well, he's the most recent person to be in charge. The whole reason she wasn't principal in the first place, apart from the fact that she was soooo much worse than me, of course, was that she treated our last Ballet Master like trash."

"You're talking about Emma Silver, right?"

"Aw, Emma's so sweet. My cousin," Kate sighed. "I miss her. I wish she had stuck around, but there were a lot of, like, bad internal politics going on because of—"

The crack of breaking glass cut across her words, and I spun away from the lake, searching for the source of the noise.

A blonde woman, tall, her long, skinny legs poking out of a pair of beige shorts stood next to one of the cars parked in front of the guesthouse. She held a tire iron in her hands, and her face was a mask of rage.

"You'll pay for this, Bernardo!" she shrieked, and brought the tire iron down on the windshield with a thwack.

Fourteen

"Hey," Kate said, with a bright smile. "That's Emma! Hey, Emma!"

I was starting to think that Kate wasn't as in touch with reality as she should've been. Emma, the previous Ballet Master, wielded the tire iron like it wasn't her first time trashing a car. She ignored Kate's greeting and brought the tire iron down a third time and then a fourth. Spidering cracks surrounded points of impact on the car's windshield.

She had chosen to take her temper out on the van bearing the words "Little Bear Ballet Company" across the side in curling fuchsia print.

Emma took a step back and then smacked the side mirror off the vehicle with relish.

"Huh," Kate said, "I wonder why she's so angry?"

I didn't grace her with an answer, but fished around in my purse for my phone. I wasn't deluded enough to think that I could take on a woman with a tire iron or that, you know, I'd get any answers out of her while she was in a rage.

I'd barely gotten my phone out of my purse when Beau appeared on the front stoop of the guesthouse. "Hey, you! Stop that! I've called the police and they're on their way. You'd better stop that right this instant or I'll—"

"Do I look like I care?" Emma shrieked, and thwacked the tire iron into the side of the van. "They've taken everything from me! Everything. This whole company, Cole, all of them are rotten to the core, and I'm going to make them pay." She continued riddling the ballet company's van with dents and breaking the windows as best she could. Her skinny arms pointed out at odd angles as she set to work, and even I had to admit she was comical in her fervor.

"You. Are. Nothing. To. Me!" Emma punctuated every word with a smack to the van.

"Emma?" Cole had appeared on the front stoop. "Emma, stop it."

"You!" She hissed, circling the van and pointing the tire iron at him.

"Oh, shoot," Kate whispered. "This isn't good."

"You've got a very firm grip on reality," I said.

Kate beamed like it was a compliment.

I started forward a step—I couldn't stand by if Emma attacked the new Ballet Master, even if he did creep me out, and even if approaching her when she was armed was inadvisable. Maybe, if I surprised her. Her back was to me, after all.

"You come down here where I can teach you a lesson," Emma said, patting the tire iron against her palm threateningly. "Don't worry, Cole, I won't mess up your pretty face or your perfect turn out."

"Turn out?" I muttered.

"His hips," Kate said, gesturing to her legs. She placed her feet in first position, pointing outward at 180 degrees. "See? Perfect turn out. Giselle could never—"

"Come down here!" Emma yelled.

"Calm down. We can talk about this," Cole said.

"I know what you did. I know you're responsible for what happened to me," she said. "And I want reparations. I want—"

"You were let go under normal circumstances, Emma. You know I had no control over that."

"Liar! Get down here."

"Has it really come to this?" Cole asked. "After everything we've been through? You don't trust my word?"

This had to be the politics Cole had mentioned during our conversation on the stoop. I was missing a key to the puzzle here, but I wasn't sure what. "What does he mean by that?" I asked Kate, hoping her vapid commentary would guide me toward the answers I sought.

"Honestly, I have no idea. I don't, like, meddle in the company's affairs. I just know that Emma was let go, and that Cole took over. But I don't know why, you know? I mean, OK, Emma was a on the abusive side, but she's a nice woman."

"Yeah," I said. "I can see that."

Kate smiled at me, not sensing my sarcasm. "She wants life to be fair, you know?"

"And I want a million dollars."

"Well, that wouldn't really be fair if you got a million dollars and—"

"Get down here!" Emma shrieked, banging the tire iron onto the hood of the car. "Get down here before I come up there."

"You'll do no such thing, ma'am," Beau said sternly, his gray hair tufting up from the breeze, and his usually friendly eyes, hard and focused. "I told you, I've called the Lake Basil Police, and they'll be here any second now, so you'd better cool your darn jets."

Faces had appeared in the windows on the second floor of the guesthouse, the ballet dancers and other guests peering down to find out what was going on. In the window of the cupola, another face appeared—instantly recognizable—Jordan, frowning down. His gaze rested on Emma for a split second and then his expression morphed into alarm. He disappeared from view.

A whooping of sirens came, and a police cruiser bumped around the corner at high speed, spitting dust from the dirt road. It skidded to a halt next to my car, barely missing it, and a police officer jumped out, drawing his gun.

"Put your hands up," he yelled. "Drop your weapon!"

Emma didn't listen to him. "Cole, get your butt down here. Don't you understand? You've taken everything from me."

"Emma, calm down," Cole said, in a warning tone.

Next to me, Kate stared, wide-eyed and started trembling. "Wait, this is really bad."

"You're only now realizing this?" I asked.

"I—I thought she was just kidding around. I — That guy really called the cops on her!" Kate started forward, and I tried catching her arm, but she was already out of reach. "Hey, wait!" She shouted. "Don't shoot her!"

The cop swung toward Kate, training his weapon on her, and I recognized him from around town. It was Carl Sager, one of the newest rookies to join the police. A thin sheen of sweat glistened on his forehead, and his Adam's apple bobbed as he swallowed. "Don't move! Don't move a step."

"Stop it," I said, and grabbed hold of Kate's arm. "You're making things worse."

"Back up. Back up right now," Carl called.

"It's OK, Carl," I said. "I've got her." And I dragged Kate backward toward the tire swing. She didn't fight me, thankfully.

Carl turned back to the tense scene, just as another person rushed out of the inn's doors.

Fifteen

"Emma, don't." Jordan rushed out onto the front stoop, one hand outstretched like he could will Emma to stop her attack on the van and on Cole.

Officer Sager trained his weapon on Jordan.

A second police cruiser came around the corner and parked, and Shawn leaped out from within, accompanied by a female officer, who had a hardened expression and her gun already out.

"Drop your weapon, ma'am." The female officer barked it out. "Ma'am, drop your weapon and back away from the car."

Emma turned her head, casting an angry gaze over her shoulder at the gathered officers.

"Emma, please," Jordan pleaded, clasping his hands

together. "Please, don't do this. We can talk about this, my love. We can—"

"Sir, be quiet," Officer Sager said.

"Drop your weapon, ma'am, and put your hands in the air," the female officer shouted.

My love? Jordan and Emma were dating? This was interesting news. How much more complicated could all of this get?

"Emma, I'm asking you to please do this," Jordan said. "For me."

Emma pointed the tire iron at Cole again. "You're lucky the cops are here, you piece of trash. If they weren't, I would've rearranged your limbs."

Eugh. What a gem.

Cole wasn't perturbed by the threat. He gave her that same soulless stare he'd given me, but didn't say a word. He remained on the stoop, waiting for whatever would take place. He didn't antagonize her, but he didn't do anything to calm her either. Maybe he'd given up because everything Cole had said earlier had only made things worse.

"Put down your weapon!"

The tension had built to a breaking point. Kate swayed beside me as if she was about to pass out, and I guided her to the grass and sat her down, patting her on the back while my gaze remained fixed on the scene.

"You're lucky," Emma said, one last time, and then dropped the tire iron in the dirt and put her hands up.

The officers rushed forward to arrest her, pinning her arms behind her back and placing her in cuffs. They didn't shove her onto the ground, and she didn't resist arrest.

I let out a breath I hadn't realized I'd been holding.

No shots fired, but one arrest and a lot of intrigue. What on earth was—?

"No! Please, leave her alone." Jordan came down the front steps, pushing past Cole who tried to stop him. "Please, she doesn't know what she's doing. She's—"

"Sir, back up right now," Officer Sager shouted, holding out a palm.

"But she doesn't know what she's doing. Look, she's innocent, OK? She's innocent." Jordan, who had clearly lost his darn mind, strode toward the officers powerfully. He tried to grab hold of Emma's arm.

Officer Sager stepped around Emma and took hold of Jordan instead. "Sir, put your hands behind your back. You're under arrest for interfering with a police officer."

"Let go of me!" Jordan shrugged the officer off, or at least he tried to. Officer Sager had a strong grip. "Hey! I'm just trying to—" He tried throwing a punch in the officer's direction, and I gasped.

Officer Sager turned him around and drove him to the ground on his stomach, immediately loosing a pair of handcuffs from his belt and slipping them onto Jordan's wrist.

What on earth was Jordan thinking? And what was going on here?

This was the second time I'd seen Jordan this emotional over something. With the death of his sister, I could understand, but directly interfering with an officer? That was a serious crime.

The officers made quick work of arresting Jordan and Emma and escorting them to separate police cruisers. Jordan didn't say a word this time, and his cheeks had gone pale, his gaze staring directly ahead as if he only now realized the error in his decision-making. Emma spat and screamed, kicking up dirt and swearing she would be back for Cole.

She had to be the murderer. Could she have blamed Giselle for her being fired as well?

The thoughts were scattered as I watched the scene unfolding. Finally, the two cruisers pulled away, and Shawn, who had been standing by to help if needed, came over. "Are you all right, Gina?"

"I'm fine," I said. "I think it's Kate who needs help. We might need to get her medical attention."

Kate was still pale, but she hadn't passed out. "No, I think I'm OK. I can't believe what happened. I—"

Shawn opened his mouth as if he wanted to say something, but a glint in the grass nearby caught my eye. I left him and Kate together, trusting that he would make sure she was all right. The glint had come from the area where Officer Sager had thrown Jordan to the ground to arrest him.

I bent and scanned the grass, frowning as I searched it.

There! A ring lay in the grass, a blade looped through its center, sparkling in the morning sunlight. It was an engagement ring, encrusted with diamonds. *It must have fallen out of Jordan's pocket, right?*

He wanted to propose to Emma? He'd called her his love, hadn't he? The question bugged me. In fact, the whole scene had bugged me.

Why was Emma so mad at Cole? And why had Jordan tried to stop her arrest? Love was one thing but—

"Gina?" Shawn talked next to me, and I rose, startled by his proximity.

He smiled at me, but the smile was taut.

"I found a ring," I said, gesturing toward the grass. "I didn't touch it in case it's evidence or something. I think it fell out of Jordan's pocket."

Shawn nodded. "Are you all right?" he asked. "You look stressed."

"I'm great. Just visiting with friends," I said, trying to scramble up an excuse as to why I was at the guest house in the first place. I didn't want Shawn getting annoyed at my interference in his case. He'd been pretty open to me poking around before, but that was when the case hadn't involved Jacob.

"You're friends with Kate?" Shawn asked, skeptically.

I turned and found that she was under the tree with the tire swing, snacking on a candy bar. Sugar for the shock maybe.

"Did you call for help?" I asked. "Medical attention?"

Shawn sighed, pinching the bridge of his nose. "Seriously, Gina. How about you let me do my job, all right? You stick to yours."

"I would if you'd give me the restaurant back," I said.

"All in good time," he replied, that tight smile returning. "Now, is there anything else you need here? I've got to talk to Beau and Mr. Bernardo. Kate too."

It was clear he wanted me to vamoose before I caused trouble. "I don't need anything from you Shawn," I said.

Sixteen

That night, I sat up in my bedroom in front of my dresser, my window open to allow in the scents of Lake Basil. Suburban smells of cooking, the fresh summer air that was scented with potential, the warmth of the sidewalk that had been baking in the sun all day. They were all comforting smells, especially coupled with the sounds of Uncle Rocco and Aunt Sofia moving around downstairs.

But I shifted.

Shifted my butt across the seat, tapping my fingers on the dressing table, my other hand closed around the hairbrush as I stared at myself in the mirror.

My eyes were bright, my hair a little on the messy, frizzy side, and my lips pursed as I critiqued myself. Not my appearance, but my thoughts and actions.

Today had been interesting to say the least.

Emma hated Cole, she had hated him so much that she had wanted to ruin the truck and had threatened him with violence. She had despised him to such a degree that when her boyfriend, Jordan, had come out onto the stoop and begged her to reconsider her actions, she had ignored him.

She had decided to do what *she* wanted to do. Why? Because she was consumed by whatever past slights Cole had exacted upon her? Or because she only cared about what she wanted?

Jordan had wanted to help Emma, and she had refused him and gone her own way, even though that way wasn't good for her.

I swallowed and put down my brush, shaking my head.

Those facts shouldn't matter, but I couldn't help obsessing over them and asking myself why? Why did I care about this relationship between two people who'd been wilding out?

I closed my eyes on the person in the mirror.

This is silly. Focus on the case.

But it all seemed intertwined. Strings that connected. Was I as selfish as Emma?

I clicked my tongue at myself and dragged my phone across the dressing table, resting it in front of me. Sitting around idly would only make things worse. I tapped on the little tab I kept open on my screen and started writing notes out.

- *Find out why Emma had a vendetta against Cole.*
- *Find out where Emma was on the night of the murder.*
- *Research more about oxycodone. How easy is it to get hold of?*
- *Draw out the table.*

I started with the last item on the list first, opening my dresser drawer and removing a pad and pen and placing them on the table.

Hastily, I sketched out the table as it had been on the night of the murder. I placed Kate opposite Giselle, Giselle beside her brother, and then Cole, the Ballet Master, on her other side.

But that was equally frustrating. Violet had told me that people had been switching seats all night.

I jotted down another note.

- *People switching places all night. At one point, Cole and Giselle went to the bathroom during the same time.*
- *Cole and Giselle were potentially dating??*
- *Kate is happy Giselle's dead.*

But as far as I knew, Kate hadn't gone anywhere *near*

the plate.

I tabbed out of my notes and opened the browser on my phone, then tapped out Cole Bernardo in the bar. The search results gave me a few hits—mainly mentions of Cole's prowess as a dancer, an announcement that he would be taking over as Ballet Master, and a few videos of him when he was younger, performing in the ballet.

His social media profile on MyBook was near the bottom of the results, but I clicked on it regardless, fascinated by all the suspects—Cole Bernardo, Emma Silver, Jordan Prentice, and Kate.

Cole had an album full of pictures dedicated to ballet on his profile. His relationship status read "SINGLE" in bold letters—interesting, since Jordan had hinted that Giselle and Cole had been seeing each other. I found a second album named "Friends and Fun" and scrolled through it. There were photos dating back for years, and—

I stopped scrolling.

One of those photos showed Cole with his arm around a much younger-looking Emma. He had her squeezed to his side, and his lips pressed against her temple. Emma leaned in to him, grinning from ear-to-ear, her fingers reaching up to touch his chin.

This was not a cute friendly picture. This was evidence of their past relationship.

Cole and Emma had dated a few years ago.

I opened a second tab and compared the ballet album to "Friends and Fun". Cole had been dancing in the ballet during Emma's time as Ballet Master, and he had been dating her. The pictures of Emma and Cole stopped about a year ago.

I scrolled furiously, switching back and forth between tabs, my heart pounding.

And then, Cole had taken over as Ballet Master six months prior. That had to be difficult for Emma to handle.

But she'd accused him of ruining her life. And there didn't appear to be any images of Cole with Giselle.

What did that mean? That he wasn't dating her? Or that he'd learned his lesson about dating someone in the ballet company?

I researched the other suspects. Jordan's MyBook profile was locked down tight. I couldn't see his albums, let alone his relationship status—though it was obvious he'd been dating Emma.

My eyes widened.

There was something there.

"Of course," I muttered. "He was dating Emma. He wanted to propose. That had to cause tension."

If Cole was Emma's ex, and Jordan was dating her now then there would have been anger and tension between the two men, right? But what on *earth* did that have to do with Giselle? Frustration bubbled through me, and I tapped my finger beside my phone.

Giselle and Jordan were related. Jordan owned a part of the Ballet Company.

Cole had dated Emma and taken over as Ballet Master about six months after their break-up.

Emma hated Cole because... he was Ballet Master? Or because he was her ex.

Jordan was now dating Emma.

I massaged my temples. This was convoluted. What did it matter about why they had broken up or who had been dating whom when it came to Giselle's death?

Giselle had died because someone wanted her gone.

The only person who had clearly disliked her was Kate, but the way she'd talked to me today—hoping the killer would get caught, talking openly about her anger at Giselle—hadn't exactly smacked of guilt. Kate seemed oblivious about implicating herself.

Maybe if I spoke to her again then I could figure this out.

There was something fishy going on with this ballet company.

I checked my notifications on my phone, just in case Jacob had messaged me, but there was nothing to show. We had chatted on and off since our date the other night, but he'd been removed of late, possibly because he sensed I was so unsure.

Guilt wormed through my belly. I would have to make a decision on how I felt soon. I wasn't the type of person who led men on. I was straight with my thoughts and feelings, and Matilda's words from the other day had been lodged in my mind for a while now.

Just how far would I go for Jacob? And—

A knock tapped at my door. Aunt Sofia was my guess. She'd mentioned watching her favorite show and wanted me to join. I slipped on my robe and got up. "Come in."

The knob turned, and Shawn Carter poked his head around the door.

Seventeen

I GASPED AND CLUTCHED MY ROBE TIGHTER around my midriff. "Uh, Shawn? What the heck?"

"Sorry, sorry," he said, dipping his gaze to the floor in my bedroom. "I should have called out first to tell you it was me."

"What are you doing here? Who let you in?" I had been so lost in thought, I hadn't heard the doorbell ringing downstairs.

"Your aunt," Shawn said. "I'll wait out in the hall until you're decent." And then he shut the door.

I stared at the back of it, shaking my head. What on earth was that about? Why was he here, upstairs, wanting to talk to me?

Let's hang around wondering about it instead of actually finding out, shall we?

I got dressed into a t-shirt and a pair of jeans, checked my hair in the mirror, and then opened the door.

Shawn immediately moved past me and into my room. Now, I wasn't a prude, and I certainly wasn't a teenager anymore, though there was still some Lake Basil High paraphernalia that I hadn't taken down in my room. I hadn't bothered since I'd figured I'd soon be moving on when I'd first come back to Lake Basil. That said, I didn't enjoy the fact that Shawn had just decided to brush past me and lay claim to my space and time like he was owed it.

I folded my arms and stared at him, tapping my foot. "Shawn," I said, "if you got something to say to me, you can call."

"This is something we need to talk about in person." He glanced down at my dressing table, where my phone lay. Thankfully, the screen had dulled from inactivity so my case notes weren't on display.

"Then why didn't you ask me to come down to the station?"

"Because this isn't related to the case," Shawn said. "Look, Gina, this is... well, it's a personal call, all right?" He scratched the back of his neck, looking sheepish. "I didn't want to interrupt you or nothing, but I... I've got to get this off my chest."

"OK? What's up?" I stopped tapping my foot.

Shawn's expression was serious, and he paced back and

forth in front of my dresser, searching around the room for words, I guessed. He smiled at the soft pink comforter lying across the end of my bed. "You always had this? Since school?"

"That's what you came to talk to me about?"

Shawn inserted a finger between his collar and throat and tugged. "Look, Gina, I don't know how you're gonna react to this, but I figured you already know what you know, so there's that—"

"I ever tell you how much I hate riddles?"

"That must be why you're always sticking your nose where it doesn't belong."

"Ha. You know, we should start a comedy club in Lake Basil. You'd make a killing. Headline act."

Shawn scratched his brow. "You're not making this any easier."

"Would you spit it out already?"

He sucked in a breath. "I love... your sense of style," he said.

I glanced down at my ratty old Lake Basil High t-shirt and then back up at him. "No, not the comedy club for you. The hospital. You need to go to the hospital."

"I— Ooh, boy." He puffed out his cheeks. "Gina, darn it, Gina, I love you. All right? There, I said it. I'm in love with you. I love you. That's how it is. That's how I feel," he said, rattling the words out. "I know you have something going on with Jacob. I know you probably don't see me the same way I see you, and I know this is the last thing you want to hear right now, but there it is. That's—Shoot, what did you expect? You came back to Lake Basil, and it was like there was... Like the whole town came to life again, and things started making sense."

My mouth had dropped open, and I stared at him, unblinking. I didn't know what to think or say.

"It's like I get you, all right? I get the person you were and who you are now, and I know we didn't maybe... We weren't best friends back then, and I've probably sent you a lot of mixed signals over the past year, but I love you. I love you. Man, I'm so friggin' soft, talking like that, but it is the way it is. I can't deny it any longer."

I finally closed my mouth and swallowed dryly. "Shawn—"

"I know," he said. "You have a boyfriend. And I'm just that annoying cop who bugs you about your restaurant. We barely talk. We haven't even hung out since you got back to town, but I can't stop thinking about you, Gina. It's like you've invaded my mind."

This was surreal.

How was I meant to respond? I didn't want to hurt Shawn's feelings, and maybe, in another life, I would have been interested in him. Or another time. Before I had gotten into a relationship with Jacob.

Before I had fallen for him.

Fallen for him? It was the first time I'd considered the big "l-word" about a man since what had happened with Larry, and it terrified me.

Meanwhile, Shawn had the guts to come up here and tell me about his feelings even though he knew I might reject him out of hand.

"You don't have to say anything," Shawn said. "I'll leave." He took a step toward me and the door that was still open and then stopped. "Actually, I'm gonna need you to say something. Please." The hope in his eyes pained me. "Give it to me straight. Real talk."

"Shawn," I said clearly. "You are a wonderful, smart man and a great cop. But I am committed to Jacob. I care about him deeply. I'm sorry."

Shawn's broad shoulders sagged. "Yeah," he said. "That's what I thought."

"I—"

"You don't have to say anything else. I heard you." His voice wasn't angry or cruel, just disappointed. "Sorry if I made you feel uncomfortable or anything like that."

"No, you didn't. Thank you."

Shawn gave a curt nod. "Yeah. I—Yeah." And then he walked out of my room. His footsteps tread heavily on the stairs, and then were gone.

I let out a breath. I could scarcely believe what had just happened.

"Are you OK, honey?" Aunt Sofia stood on the threshold of my room. "Do you want me to get you something sweet? Might help for the shock."

I couldn't answer her. I'd thought that the case was complicated. Turned out, that was just my life. I couldn't go on living in a state of confusion, and I had taken my first step toward clarifying things. I had chosen Jacob because it was the right thing to do. Because I cared about him too.

Aunt Sofia came over and put her arms around me, giving me a squeeze. She was a little shorter than me, but she smelled so familiar—of her favorite rosy perfume and the scent of baking. A warm, nurturing scent that made me feel small and protected again.

I hugged her back. "Thanks, Auntie."

"Come on downstairs and have something to eat. I made brownies. The sugar will help."

It felt like the only thing that would help would be clearing Jacob's name and opening the restaurant again.

Eighteen

The following morning...

There wasn't much to do with the restaurant closed, apart from normal administrative tasks. The cops were quiet about when I would be able to open it again, and that was frustrating me to no end. So Aunt Sofia, in her eternal wisdom, gave me a list of groceries to pick up from the bodega and strict instructions not to come back until I'd had a coffee and picked my lip up off the floor.

I opted for Cara's Coffee Shop, which was just around the corner from the restaurant, because I could soak up the atmosphere, pick up the gossip, and head over to Matilda's right after obsessing over the case.

All in a day's... worry.

Cara's Coffee had a cozy atmosphere that drew in all the locals at every hour of the day—wooden counters, music playing from the stereo, and a couple of hanging potted plants to accent the space. It helped that the coffee shop served ready to made croissants and sandwiches for hungry customers as well. What didn't help was that Brittany Brown was behind the counter today.

Brittany, with her platinum blonde hair tied back in a long ponytail and her makeup done to perfection, served the customers with a greeting and a smile. She'd taken up a permanent position at Cara's Coffee since her divorce from her rich husband, but it hadn't put a damper on her penchant for dissing anybody who got on her bad side.

And since I was the target of her high school bullying back in the day, I was most definitely on her list.

I joined the long line that wound through the coffee shop, enjoying the hum of people talking and the coolness from the air-conditioning unit that puttered in the corner of the room. Lake Basil was heading toward all-time highs this summer, and I was kind of looking forward to it. I'd never been a "boating" kind of gal, but I might give it a shot this year.

The queue moved, and I caught sight of Brittany, tossing her hair and talking loudly to the customer who'd stepped up to be served next.

"—of course, yeah," she said. "I mean, everybody's heard about it at this point. It's a *huge* deal."

The customer replied in an undertone.

Brittany let out a foghorn laugh. "As if. I mean, if anybody thinks it's Jacob, they're crazy," she said. "He's a good guy, even if he works for the wrong person."

I rolled my eyes heavenward. Jacob had been Brittany's brother-in-law, and I was pretty sure she had a crush on him, even though that was mighty weird in my books.

"Besides, everybody saw what happened on opening night," she said. "Yeah, the ballet. They nearly called the police."

A few people in front of me muttered and shifted, irritated at being made to wait while Brittany had a fat chat with the customer at the front of the line.

"Because that Giselle girl, the one that died, nearly strangled her!" A pause. "The lady with the blonde hair, yeah. I don't know her name, but there's a rumor going around that she was arrested and—"

"Excuse me," a man in front of me called out. "Can you hurry up, please? Some of us got a job to get to."

Brittany rolled her eyes at him, but finished up her conversation with the customer. The queue shifted forward again shortly after that, but I wasn't at the front yet. Which meant I had plenty of time to consider Brittany's new piece of gossip.

Giselle and "the blonde-haired woman who had been arrested" had gotten into a fight after the opening night of the ballet. That had to mean that the victim had been fighting with Emma, who just happened to be engaged to Giselle's brother.

It was a tenuous connection between the two.

I'd already figured out that Cole and Emma had been dating and that Cole had replaced Emma as Ballet Master. That gave Emma plenty of reason to hate Cole, but with Giselle being the one that had been murdered...

I reached the front of the line, and my thoughts were cut off by Brittany's vicious stare.

"Pizzaface Romano," she said, smirking. "So, you thought you'd stop by to—"

"Regular coffee to go, please." I didn't have time for her shenanigans today. I had to jot down what I was thinking. I grabbed a napkin while I waited.

"Pizzaface, you really think you can—" Brittany started, handing over the drink.

I took it, dropped money on the counter and then walked over to a comfy armchair next to one of the quaint wooden tables. Brittany called out something after me, but I ignored her. Instead, I removed a pen from my pocket and started scribbling on the napkin, inspired by what I'd heard.

Connections. This is all about connections. I just have to riddle them out.

I pressed lightly as I wrote, careful not to rip the napkin apart in my furious brainstorming.

Connections:

Cole→ dated and took over the ballet from→Emma (angry, arrested for attacking truck and wanting to attack Cole)

Emma→ dating and soon-to-be engaged to→Jordan (lovesick puppy dog, but Emma didn't seem as invested as he was when the arrest happened?)

Jordan→brother and highly protective over→Giselle (vegan, poisoned by oxycodone)

Giselle→fought with→Emma (who hates Cole who replaced Kate with Giselle), Kate (who was the principal when Kate was in charge)

So, that had to mean that the main suspects in the case were... Kate and Emma, right? Emma had already shown that she was more than willing to get violent if necessary, and Kate had shown that she didn't particularly enjoy Giselle's company.

But Kate had been sitting on the opposite side of the table to Giselle, and that would have made poisoning her plate darn near impossible.

And Emma? She hadn't even been in the restaurant, so

poisoning the plate wasn't just darn near impossible, it was *actually* impossible. Physically so.

Also, Emma had appeared to be the type to deal with her problems in a hands-on manner, if her confrontation with Cole was anything to go by. Whereas poison was... well, it was the coward's route. It was a way to kill someone while avoiding that direct confrontation.

I scratched my chin, studying the napkin.

There was something *not right* about all of this. I could understand Kate hating Giselle, and I could even stretch toward Giselle and Emma having a falling out because of what had happened at the ballet the other night, but murder? For that?

I needed to talk to someone about this. Thankfully, I had just the woman in mind.

Nineteen

Matilda came out from behind the counter, drying her hands on her apron, and came over, a frown wrinkling her brow. "What's going on, Gina?"

"Huh?" I looked up from my napkin.

I'd finished my coffee, a cup of tea, and a slice of carrot cake ages ago, and had been staring at the connections I'd made for so long that my eyes burned from the intense concentration. Or the lack of blinking.

Jumbo sat curled in my lap, though I hadn't realized he'd transferred from the sunny chaise lounge to where I sat at my favorite table beside it. The bakery was quiet, with a few customers dotted around the cutesy interior.

"You've been rocking back and forth and muttering under your breath for a half an hour," Matilda said. "No offense, but my customers are starting to, uh, stare."

I licked my lips and glanced around. And, indeed, there were a few people watching me warily or studying me over the rims of their tea cups.

"Sorry," I laughed, brushing a hand over my hair. "Sorry, I'm trying to figure this out. I can't get to the bottom of it, no matter how hard I try. I was waiting for your break so we could talk about it."

"I'm on my break now," Matilda said. "Let's go upstairs and talk for a half hour. Maybe I can help you work it out."

"You're the best." I moved Jumbo off my lap, and he gave me a protest meow-purr as a reward, then got up, taking my napkin and purse with me. Thinking about the case and the connections was a great way to avoid thinking about Shawn and Jacob.

I followed Matilda upstairs, and she settled me as she always did—on the sofa with a refreshment. She flopped down in the armchair opposite mine.

"OK," she said. "So, what's going on? I've never seen you this obsessed before. Not even when there was this type of *thing* happening last year." She shivered at the memory of the past murders that had rocked Lake Basil.

I let out a breath and then launched into my tale, telling her about the evidence I'd picked up on, as well as the tenuous connections I'd made between everyone.

Matilda listened, wriggling her nose from side-to-side occasionally.

I drew in a deep breath once I was done.

"Huh," Matilda said, under her breath.

"What?"

"It seems really complicated. And what about the oxycodone?" Matilda asked.

"What about it?"

"Have you considered where that might have come from?" she asked. "It seems to me that it might be the key to figuring it all out. Oxycodone is a *really* strong painkiller. Only somebody who was in an accident or is really sick would need something like that, and the murderer must have had easy access to it."

"You're right," I said. "But figuring that out isn't easy. I haven't seen anything from the suspects that might suggest any of them needed a prescription like that." I shifted on the sofa, tucking my legs underneath my body. "A painkiller. A painkiller."

But no matter how often I repeated it, it didn't get me any closer to the truth.

"So, here's what you're saying." Matilda rose and walked toward her TV, pacing in front of it. "First, that the only people who seem to have a motive to kill Giselle were either at the opposite end of the table or not even in the restaurant?"

"Correct."

"And that the food was brought out while Giselle wasn't at the table?" Matilda asked.

"That's what Violet said. She said that Giselle and Cole had gotten up from the table at some point, and it was after the food came."

"But Giselle got up a second time, claiming she was sick, after she had tasted the food."

"She also said that she was sure it contained meat," I said. "Which it didn't."

"And she didn't take a bite of it after she got it back from the kitchen?"

"No, she didn't. Jordan and Giselle continued lambasting me, and then Jacob came out to talk to them right after," I said. "Giselle didn't eat any more of it."

Matilda massaged the spot between her eyebrows. "OK. That *is* confusing. Why was Giselle getting up to go to the bathroom that much?"

"The first time might have been just because she needed to go, you know? The second time was because she was sick, and from what Violet said, and from what I saw, a lot of the guests were getting up and moving around throughout the evening. They were having a regular party," I said.

Matilda started pacing again, and my gaze wandered to the window and the view of the top of my building across the street. I could just make out the "R" in Romano's from this angle.

"So everybody's moving around."

"Except for Kate," I said. "She stayed where she was."

"So it couldn't have been her then," Matilda said. "Or your other suspect."

"See my problem with this whole thing?"

"Have you considered the brother?" Matilda asked.

"I have, but I just don't see it. Why would Jordan, who co-owned the company, who was dating Emma and loved her, and who adored his sister to the point where he obsessed over her staying vegan, kill his beloved sister at a table full of people?" I asked.

"And the Ballet Master?" Matilda asked.

"I guess," I said, "but at the same time, he didn't have much of a motive. It seemed like he got on with Giselle. And while he didn't like Jordan or vice versa, that anger or hatred didn't seem to transfer to Giselle. Besides, Cole chose Giselle to replace Kate. I guess there's some ballet company politics I'm not seeing here, but I don't get how that factors into what happened to her."

"She was the principal dancer, right? So the politics had to affect her," Matilda said, but even she had a hint of doubt in her tone. "I think."

"I don't know." I was out of ideas unless you counted the oxycodone, but it wasn't like I could go to the drug store and ask who'd fulfilled a prescription for it. First, I wasn't a cop, and second, these dancers weren't native to Lake Basil. It wasn't like someone had gotten their prescription in town. For all I knew, they could have gotten it out of town or in a different state entirely.

I lay back on the sofa, shutting my eyes for a second.

Matilda moved nearby, and when I peeked at her through one eye, she was beside her window that overlooked the sunny street below. She made a strange noise in her throat, grasping at the flowery apron stretched over her stomach.

"What is it?" I asked.

"The camera," she said, turning toward me with a triumphant smile on my face, pointing to the black bulb on her window sill. "My new camera! You don't think it might have... caught something, do you?"

Twenty

"You're a genius, Matilda!" I slung an arm around her shoulders and hugged her to my side. "You are an actual genius. I can't believe this."

Matilda laughed at my enthusiasm. "I'm going to pull it up for you real quick and then I have to head back downstairs. My break is over, but feel free to hang around up here and go over the footage."

"Thank you!" I was super excited about this because it felt like a break in the case, even though I hadn't even seen what was on the footage yet.

Matilda had set up her laptop on the sofa, and she opened it, then brought up the app that was connected to her camera. "OK, so you should be able to find the footage from that night in this folder here. Just go through it and that's it. Let me know if you need anything else, OK?"

"You're the best!"

She laughed again, tucking her graying hair behind one ear. "Thanks, Gina, but I'm just a security conscious, nosy people-watcher. Let's not get ahead of ourselves here."

I couldn't help giving her another giddy smile.

Matilda swept from the apartment, the dull hum of people talking downstairs swelling and then muting as she opened and closed the door.

I clicked on the folder bearing the date of our soft launch and started going through the footage. It was chopped into six-hour pieces, so I could skim over earlier in the night and focus on the part from where the guests had arrived until they had left.

The view of the restaurant was clear.

I could make out the table inside, and even my legs as I moved back and forth, preparing for the arrival of the guests. There was also the street view of the front of Romano's and the sidewalk out front.

I trawled through the video, my mouth dry and my shoulders tense, hoping against hope that I would finally find something.

My heart leaped as the first guests pulled up and got out of their cars. The last to arrive was Giselle and—

I gasped.

Giselle emerged from Jordan's fancy red sports car—

now wrecked—and was followed by Jordan himself and... Emma!

I noted down the time as 06:00 p.m. and let the video play, wishing that there was sound even though that obviously wasn't possible.

Jordan walked toward the front of the restaurant and stopped, turning back toward the two women. Emma moved to join him, but Giselle put out a hand and stopped her. The two women turned toward each other, glaring, and looking angry enough to hiss and spit.

Jordan appeared to be trying to placate them, patting the air, even clasping his hands together in a gesture that said he was begging for them to get along.

It didn't work.

Emma raised a fist. Giselle backed up a step, shaking her head, her expression defiant rather than afraid.

Why were they arguing? What was this about?

This meant that Emma had been around the restaurant on that night, even though she hadn't been inside it. Was it possible that she had somehow slipped through a bathroom window or the kitchen or something and poisoned Giselle's food?

There was a tense moment when nothing happened, and I was almost certain that the screen was frozen, and then the front door opened and Kate emerged.

She said something that broke the tension, and Emma lowered her fist.

Giselle and Jordan entered together, while Kate lingered outside, talking to her old Ballet Master who was clearly her friend. The two exchanged a few words and then Emma handed something to Kate that I couldn't quite make out.

"That's it! It has to be the oxycodone!"

Emma left on foot. Kate returned to the restaurant.

I cut off the footage, my pulse racing at what I'd witnessed. This had to be the definitive evidence I needed that proved Kate had done the deed. Not only did it show that both Jacob and I, and the entire kitchen staff, were all innocent of the crime, but Emma had been at the restaurant that evening.

And she was buddy-buddy with Kate, who *hated* the victim. It made sense that they would team up together to take her down.

They were the only two who'd despised her, so they both had motives. Where I couldn't prove that one of them had done it, maybe I could prove that they'd teamed up.

My excitement threatened to overwhelm me, and I paused the video, trembling all over.

I needed to do a few things first. Make a copy of the video was at the top of the list. Send that video to Shawn was next up—he had no idea that Matilda had a camera, since she hadn't even thought about it until now. I didn't blame her with how busy she'd been at the bakery. And then, I had to talk to Kate about what had happened.

I needed to know what Emma had given her.

If I could clarify that, then I was that much closer to solving the case.

The only problem was finding out that information without letting Kate know I was onto her being a part of the plot to murder Giselle. It was tempting to just leave it to Shawn, but I couldn't stop now, not when I was inches from the truth.

I set to work making a quick copy of the video and transferring it to the flash drive I carried in my purse, just in case, and then rose from my seat, determination thrumming through me.

If I played my cards right, I could have the restaurant up and running and Giselle's murderers behind bars before the end of the day.

Was it too much to hope?

Twenty-One

Nerves built in my belly as I directed my Honda along the bumpy road that encircled Lake Basil. The sun glimmered on the water, trees dipping their leaf-laden branches toward the surface of the lake as if they were just as desperate to be out of the heat as the rest of the residents of our town.

Today's temperature had soared higher than anticipated, and it made everything I was doing more difficult—there was an almost molasses quality to how things ran in Lake Basil when it was hot.

I parked my car outside the Lake Basil Guesthouse, my heart murmuring doubts.

What if I was wrong about this? What if Shawn got here and decided I was out of line for coming all this way to ask Kate questions?

Even worse, what if he hadn't read my message in the first place because he was angry about our conversation the other day? I'd hurt him, even though it hadn't been my intention.

Now isn't the time to worry about complicated relationship dynamics. But there was nothing complicated to worry about. Shawn was a kind, amazing man, but he wasn't *my* kind, amazing man. Jacob was.

I got out of the Honda and bumped the door closed with my hip, scanning the parked cars out front. The van bearing the ballet company's name was gone. The doors to the guesthouse were closed today, likely because Beau wanted to keep the cool in and the heat out.

Let's do this.

Inside the guesthouse, Beau was at the reception desk as always. He offered me a warm smile, brushing a handkerchief over his forehead. "Back so soon, Gina? You want to book a room? We're full until Shawn solves that case, you know, since these ballet company people can't leave town until he does. Darn ballet idiots." Beau muttered the last part under his breath.

"Having trouble with them, Beau?"

"Trouble? If that's what you wanna call it. I'm having trouble like I have a bad back. It's just a thing I've got, doesn't matter who stays in the guesthouse or not."

I flashed him a smile. Heat and Beau didn't mingle, apparently. "Is Kate around? The redhead."

"Sure. Probably. I think I saw her head out onto the enclosed stoop earlier. You should check through there." Beau gestured toward an open doorway to his left. The inside of the guesthouse was wood-floored with floral wallpaper and white wainscoting—cute and comforting. Cool, compared to outside.

I walked out onto the enclosed stoop—windows looked out on the lake, the tire swing, and the green grass—and found Kate seated at one of the tables, a book open in one hand. She dabbed sweat from her forehead and looked up at me. Her eyes brightened. "Oh, hey! Gina, right?"

"Right," I said. "How are you, Kate?"

"Been better, been worse," she laughed. "What brings you out here again?"

"Well," I said, "I wanted to talk to you about a couple of things."

"All right." She shut her book on her thumb and smiled at me. I wasn't sure what this girl's deal was, but she gave off a serious airhead vibe. My perception of her was colored by our past encounter, where she'd been totally OK with Emma trashing the ballet company's vehicle.

"You're close with Emma, right?"

"Sure," she said, then grimaced. "Is this about what

happened the other day? I felt bad for her, you know? I don't think she was in her right mind or whatever. She was emotional because of stuff."

"You mean because of how things went down with the ballet company. The fact that she wasn't the Ballet Master anymore?"

"Sure. Yeah."

"I'm not here to talk about that incident," I said. "I wanted to ask you about the night that Giselle died."

"How come?"

"Because the cops think that my chef killed her," I said. "And they've closed down my restaurant. Also because I'm genuinely curious about what happened to the girl. We all witnessed her death. It was disturbing."

"OK?"

Apparently not that disturbing for Kate. "So, I'm trying to figure this out myself," I said. "And I would appreciate your help."

"Oh." Kate patted her book against her lap.

"I have video footage of you on the night you were at the restaurant. You came out to greet Jordan and Emma," I said. "Because they're dating, right?"

Kate shrugged. "I guess. I mean, everybody knows that. So what?"

"Emma didn't come into the restaurant. Do you know why?"

"Because Giselle didn't want her to," Kate said simply. "And because Cole didn't neither. Emma didn't like the ballet company after she got replaced. She caused a lot of trouble. She's been following us for months, even though she was fired." Kate shook her head. "Which is totally not fair since she's not a bad person. Just misunderstood."

"She's lucky she has such a loyal cousin," I said.

A cousin that would support her even when she was so clearly in the wrong.

"Emma gave you something that night. You took it inside the restaurant. What was it?" I asked.

Kate stopped tapping the book in her lap. "How do you know that?"

"I've got security camera footage of it happening," I said. "Of Emma handing you something. I've forwarded that footage to the cops as well, so you may as well tell me the truth, Kate. What did Emma give you?"

"It was just some meds," she said.

"Meds?"

"Yeah, like drugs. Meds. Not the illegal kind, the usual kind." Kate's shoulders had tensed, and her green eyes were bright and focused on me. The haze of ditziness had cleared somewhat. Was it an act?

"Why did she give you meds? What were they?"

"It was nothing serious. Just some aspirin for a headache," Kate said. "Not for me or anything. For

Jordan. He's been having a lot of headaches recently, so she asked me to give them to him."

"And did you?" I asked.

There was a world in which Kate didn't realize that the drugs she'd been given had actually been oxycodone. The same oxycodone that had killed Giselle. Though why Giselle's own caring brother, who had been so distraught he'd crashed his car over her, would have wanted to kill her was a question for later examination.

Kate shook her head sheepishly. "Nah. I kind of forgot. I left them in my purse."

"So you still have them then?"

"Nope," she said. "I lost them. They weren't in there the next morning."

"Wait, what? You lost them?"

"Yeah."

"How?" I asked. "How did you just *lose* them? Surely, you must have—"

A black SUV pulled up outside the house, and Shawn emerged from within, his identification hanging around his neck. My heart tugged and pulled strangely in my chest at the sight of him standing there. He didn't look forlorn or hard-done-by, but my thoughts immediately turned to how hurt he'd been by my rejection.

"I don't know," Kate said, cutting across my thoughts. "They just weren't in there when I looked the next day."

"One last thing," I said, as Shawn started approaching the guesthouse. "Do you know why Emma stopped being Ballet Master? Why was she replaced?"

"Nope." Kate's lips clammed together, her gaze darting nervously toward the door to the enclosed stoop.

Shawn entered and stopped dead. "Gina," he said. "Let's talk."

Twenty-Two

"Detective Carter," I said, rising from my seat. "How are you today, sir?"

"Gina." He beckoned. "Step out into the hall with me for a second."

I was confused. He'd come all this way just to talk to me? Or was this just so he could talk to me before he approached Kate about what I'd sent him.

In the hall, Shawn walked me away from the stoop but kept the door to it within view. The inn was full of light from outside, and marginally cooler. The scent of Shawn's cologne enveloped me, and I couldn't help being comforted by it and confused. Why did I like it? Was it wrong that I thought Shawn was a good guy?

I didn't need mixed feelings right now. Things were

tough enough as it was without throwing that into the ring.

"Shawn?" I frowned up at him. "Why are we out here talking instead of you being in there talking to the suspect?"

"I've told you in the past that I appreciate your help," he said. "But that's got to stop now."

"Why?"

"Because you're stepping out of line. I appreciate you sending me the video, that is great information and good to know, but coming here and questioning Kate was not it," Shawn said.

I stared at him, wanting to argue, but he was right. I was technically getting in his way. "You never had a problem with me interfering before."

"That's a lie and you know it, Gina. I did have a problem. I just walked it back because I—Nevermind."

"Because you had feelings for me," I said. "So me being able to look into this type of stuff was conditional. It depends on how I feel about you? Is that it?"

"No," Shawn said. "No. It's not about how you *feel*. It's about me doing the wrong thing because of how I feel. Felt."

I swallowed. There was that word again. Feel. Why did everything have to be about that?

"I'm trying to save my restaurant and clear—"

"Your boyfriend's name," Shawn said, with a hint of bitterness. "Trust me, I know. And I've got this under control."

"If you had it under control, why didn't you question the people who live and work in the buildings up and down the street where the murder happened to hear what they had to say about the night it—"

"I did," he said. "Matilda didn't tell me anything about the camera."

I gritted my teeth and folded my arms.

"It's time for you to move along, Gina," he said. "I've got work to do here. Got it?"

"Got it." I snapped and marched off, my cheeks blazing, hating how irrational this made me feel. It was silly to be mad at Shawn for doing his job. I had been relying on his good will to get away with my own "investigation." That was fine. I'd have to be more careful going forward.

Because I wasn't going to let Shawn Carter tell me that I couldn't keep looking into this mystery. I was hooked now, and I was so close to finding the truth, I could almost taste it.

IN A STROKE OF POOR TASTE OR GENIUS, THE JURY was still out on that one, Aunt Sofia had decided to make cannelloni for dinner. She said recent events had inspired her, to which I'd asked if her plan was to off Uncle Rocco and me. The horror on her face had been so comical, it had been worth the off-color joke.

Besides, comedy was the only way I could lighten my mood after my encounter with Shawn earlier in the day.

I finished my cannelloni in the living room, barely taking in the game on the TV or Uncle Rocco's frustrated rumblings as he watched. Aunt Sofia was on the phone, talking to one of her friends from the salon, and the occasional gasp or bout of laughter traveled down the hall.

My fork scraped my plate, and I set it aside, thinking hard.

Kate had taken meds from Emma to give to Jordan. Either Emma had actually given Kate aspirin, or it had been something else. I leaned toward the latter because the meds were missing from Kate's purse, and she *allegedly* didn't know where they'd gone.

Either that was a lie or...

Ugh. This was difficult to piece together.

If Emma had given Kate oxycodone, then that had to mean that either Emma was involved in the murder or that Jordan had taken part. But that didn't add up. I could see why Emma would want to get rid of Giselle, but not Jordan.

And how had Emma gotten hold of oxycodone in the first place? She would have needed a prescription.

A prescription from a doctor. Could Emma have had some kind of issue that had caused her firing from position as Ballet Master? It was the only thing that made sense. And I could see her being angry with Cole for taking her place, especially after them having been in a relationship.

I cleared up the plates in the living room then trudged upstairs, working the puzzle over in my mind again and again.

I opened a browser tab on my phone and typed in "Little Bear Ballet Company." I had researched some of this before, but all I knew thus far was that Jordan was a *co-owner*. So, who was the other owner?

I scrolled down the page until I found the "About Us" tab and tapped on it, taking a seat at my dressing table.

There was a number at the bottom of the page. I dialed it, hoping that this wasn't Jordan's personal cellphone.

"Hello?" A woman croaked on the other end of the line.

"Hi," I said. "I'm looking for the Little Bear Ballet Company."

"Yeah, you've found us. This is Allegra speaking," she said. "Do you want to book us for an event or are you interested in buying tickets for our performance in New York City? We've pushed the date back but—"

"Are you the receptionist?" I asked.

"Weird question, lady, but no. I'm the owner."

"Oh," I said. "Then I have a question for you."

"All right. Fire away. It's not like I got other stuff to do," she said dryly.

"What happened to Emma? Why did she get replaced as the Ballet Master? I really enjoyed watching the shows that she directed."

"Ah, I understand," Allegra said, in rasping tones. "But, you see, there was an unfortunate incident. Emma had to be replaced."

"Which incident?"

"She was in a car crash. Messed her leg up pretty bad. She was off work for a couple of months, and, real talk, the show had to go on," Allegra continued. "It is what it is, know what I'm saying? We've got a great Ballet Master who—"

"So she was in an accident," I said. "Was she driving under the influence?"

"Look, lady, your questions are weird."

"I just want—"

Allegra hung up on me, but I didn't care. I'd found out what I needed to know. Emma had most definitely been in an accident. I'd figured it had been ballet-related, but I had been wrong. Emma had been injured badly enough to get a prescription of oxycodone. Or she'd already had the oxycodone and had crashed because of it.

Either way, I was fairly certain I understood where the drug had come from. Now, I just had to prove it. And figure out *why* Jordan or Emma had poisoned Giselle in the first place.

Twenty-Three

Later that night...

I LAY ON MY BED, MY LAPTOP ON MY STOMACH, the flash drive poking from its side, and tapped on the screen, going over the footage of Emma handing Kate the package of *something*—the aspirin, according to Kate—before leaving the sidewalk outside of Romano's.

The more I turned it over in my mind, the more convinced I was that this video was the key to proving Jordan and Emma had worked together to get rid of Giselle. I didn't understand why. Furthermore, I couldn't grasp how they'd thought they would get away with this.

Maybe, they'd meant to poison Giselle lightly, just enough so that she wouldn't be able to perform? Or that she'd get sick enough to get booked off by a doctor? Or had they wanted to kill her and blame it on the food?

"But why?" I murmured, clicking again. "Why? Why, why? Why kill her in the first place?"

It was plain that Cole had taken over Emma's spot because he was the most qualified for the position, and that it had happened after their break-up, and after Emma had crashed and hurt herself, rendering her incapable of fulfilling her duties as Ballet Master.

I shut my eyes and tried to relax, but it was nearly impossible. I'd tried sleeping, and my restless mind hadn't let me. Relaxing went about the same.

There had to be a way to figure this out.

It all led back to Emma and the oxycodone, didn't it?

A text blipped through on my phone, and I opened my eyes, lifting my cellphone off the nightstand and to my face. The text message was from Jacob.

Hey. Thinking about you. I haven't heard from you all day.

Gosh, I had been so wrapped up in wanting to make sure Jacob didn't take the fall for the crime that I hadn't been messaging him or talking to him.

Miss you. I shot the message back. *Just about to go to bed. Been a long day. Are you OK?*

Sure. See you tomorrow? Coffee?

I hesitated. Tomorrow?

Sounds good. I sent it back, even though I wasn't sure I wanted to see anyone at the moment. It had been a confusing time, and while I was committed to Jacob, I struggled to keep my mind clear of worries and doubts.

My gaze wandered back to the screen, and I let the section of video play again, watching as Kate emerged and Emma handed her the meds for what had to be the hundredth time.

I let the video play on this time, watching as the customers disappeared into the restaurant.

I could make out my legs moving back and forth, walking through the restaurant to get everyone seated and learn their names. The bottom halves of Violet and Charles were also visible as they navigated the table taking orders.

The diners were seated so that I could make them out, their top halves cut from view, but their clothes identifying them. I couldn't see their hands moving, unless they were under the table and in view of the camera's angle.

Giselle was sitting next to her brother, Jordan, and Cole was on her other side.

I frowned.

Wait, that was wrong.

I remembered Giselle sitting next to Jordan, talking to Cole, yes, but then later, hadn't she been sitting next to

Cole, while Jordan was beside him? Or was that just my exhaustion talking?

I forwarded the video to see if I was right.

Cole and Giselle talked for ages. Kate remained where she was throughout the evening, and—

"There!"

Giselle and Cole had gotten up to go to the bathroom, just as Violet had told me. And when they returned to the table, instead of taking their seats the same as before, Cole sat in Giselle's place and vice versa. And Cole's plate was in front of Giselle.

So that had to mean that Cole had eaten from Giselle's plate, and Giselle from Cole's. And if that was the case, then...

Then the food that had killed Giselle had been meant for Cole.

The realization was so momentous that I expected an audible click to sound out in my small childhood bedroom.

The food had been meant for Cole. The person who had poisoned that food had wanted to get rid of Cole, not Giselle.

And the only individual who might've had those drugs was Kate? Or maybe Jordan?

Jordan had despised Cole. There was no love lost between those two, and then there was the fact that Jordan was co-owner of the ballet company, that he was dating the now-fired Ballet Master, Emma, who had also once dated Cole.

A series of consecutive clicks went off in my mind.

Cole was the target. Cole was the one Jordan had wanted to get rid of, possibly because he wanted his girlfriend, the one he had been willing to charge the cops for, to be the Ballet Master again.

No wonder Jordan had been so distraught over his sister's passing. And he had crashed into the back of the forensic van.

He had also thrown himself at a police officer for Emma. He had wanted to protect her from the consequences of her own actions. It would have been sweet if not for the fact that they were both totally crazy.

They had tried to kill Cole and had murdered Giselle instead.

I grabbed my phone again, my heart beating a mile a minute, and then sent a message to Shawn, my fingers shaking as I typed them out.

"Go to 04:03:15 in the video. They wanted to kill Cole!" And then I shifted the laptop and got out of bed, unable to sit still.

Cole and Jordan were both at the Lake Basil Guesthouse right now. That meant that the murderer and his intended victim were in the same space. That was a recipe for disaster. If I was right about this, Jordan, in his anger about Emma's arrest and everything else that had happened, might decide now was the right time to get rid of his target.

I had to get down there before it was too late.

Twenty-Four

I PARKED MY CAR IN FRONT OF THE GUESTHOUSE as I'd done plenty of times over the past little while. The difference was, this time, it was dark, and there were only a few lights on inside. And I was so nervous, my hands were slick with sweat.

Things could go wrong easily, but I'd done my due diligence, right? I'd told Shawn about what I'd found.

Besides, if I discovered any other pivotal evidence, I would simply call him over here.

I got out of the Honda into the balmy evening air, the scent of the lake and the greenery doing nothing to soothe me this evening. It wasn't too late—just past 08:00 p.m.—and I had to hope that the front doors of the guesthouse were unlocked.

I hurried up the steps and tried them.

Locked.

I knocked softly on the door. Footsteps approached it, and it cracked open to reveal Beau's smiling face. "Oh, Gina! What are you doing here?"

"Sorry to bother you, Beau," I said. "I'm stopping by to check on a friend of mine. Uh, Kate. Is she around?"

"Oh, sure, sure. She's gone up to her room on the second floor," Beau said.

"Mind if I come in?"

"No problem," he said. "She know you're visiting?"

"It's a surprise." I smiled at him.

He nodded. "She needs a good one after what happened earlier. She left with Shawn Carter, you know. Had to go down to the station to talk to him about that murder." Beau grimaced. "Anyways, up on the second floor."

"Is that where all the ballet company guests are staying."

"Yeah," he said. "For the most part. Jordan's in the attic room. He wanted the top spot in the house."

"Oh," I said. "That's something."

"Guy's got a real ego problem if you ask me," Beau said. "But that's none of my business." He waved me off, heading on down the hall toward the open plan dining room.

The guest house was cozy, and the wooden stairs

creaked underfoot as I ascended two flights. On the second floor, I searched around for the staircase that would take me up to the attic. The stairs had a varnished balustrade and spiraled upward to a trap door that was shut.

It was quaint, but it also made my stomach want to fold over on itself.

What if the trap door was locked? If someone caught me in the act...

I didn't let my doubts stop me. Instead, I strode down the hall as if I belonged in it and took the stairs two at a time. I tried the trap door and found it locked.

Darn. Now what?

Call Beau up and ask him to open it for me? Yeah, I doubted his hospitable nature would extend that far.

There had to be *something* I could do.

The trapdoor had an old brass keyhole, and the outline seated against the wooden ceiling showed a gap where the tumbler sat, exposed. I wasn't a pro-lock picker, but I did have my purse on me. And my business credit card.

I scrambled it out, going for broke. If I could find evidence in Jordan's room, that would be everything we needed. And it wasn't like the police could search it without a warrant. They needed probable cause, right? I could give them that, even if I got in trouble for trespassing. It wouldn't be the first time I hadn't stuck to the rules when it came to investigating these cases.

I inserted the card through the gap between the trap door and the ceiling and fumbled around, trying to get the door open.

My card bent under the pressure of my fiddling, then promptly shot out of my fingers and through the crack in the trapdoor, landing with a plastic clatter on the other side.

"Noooo," I hissed. "Oh, no, no, no." That was possibly one of the worst things that could have happened.

The thought had barely formed in my mind when Jordan rounded the corner down below and found me, standing with my fingers pressed against the trapdoor in horror at having lost my credit card.

OK, so I was wrong. This is the worst thing that could have happened.

Jordan stopped dead in his tracks, narrowing his eyes at me. "Hey! What do you think you're doing?"

"Jordan?" I lowered my hands and put on a big smile. "Hi, how are you?"

"What are you doing trying to get into my room?"

"Your room?" I frowned. "Oh, man. I thought this was Kate's room. I was just trying to knock when I heard a noise from inside. I swear I heard someone call for help."

Jordan jerked back a step. "That's impossible. There's no one up there."

"Just telling you what I heard," I said. "I started trying to get in because I was sure that Kate needed my help."

"You're sure you heard someone up there?" Jordan asked, rushing over.

"Positive." I scooched to the side of the balustrade, barely able to breathe now that I was in the presence of an actual murderer.

Jordan removed his key from his pocket, giving me a broody look that would have been handsome on a man who hadn't killed his own sister and might have plans to kill again. He unlocked the door then climbed the set of steps that extended from the trap door.

My card dropped down from above, and I swept it up hastily, relief bursting in my chest.

I didn't follow Jordan up. I didn't want to be trapped in the attic with a monster. Besides, I wasn't about to find the evidence I needed with him in the room.

"There's no one up here," Jordan said, looking down at me from above. "You're sure you heard something."

"Positive," I said. "Maybe it was the TV. Anyway, do you know which room Kate is in? I actually came to visit her. I must've gotten mixed up by Beau's directions."

Jordan gave me a suspicious look. "Why don't you come on up and check whether there's anyone in the room?"

"Huh? No, I'm good. I believe you. I must have

misheard." Nerves fluttered through my belly. I didn't like the look on his face. A coldness had come over him. A certainty.

I took several steps away, my back hitting the balustrade. "I'll get going now."

Jordan jumped down from above, not even bothering to use the steps. He grabbed hold of my arm, his lips peeling back over his teeth. "I'm afraid I can't let you do that," he said.

Twenty-Five

"Let go of me," I commanded. "Right now."

"You're not going anywhere," Jordan repeated, his grip on my arm tightening. "You said you heard something in my room, so you're going to come upstairs and check. I'm not letting you leave until you do."

"You can't restrict my movements," I said. "And I'm not going anywhere with you."

What was the rule? Something along the lines of "never let them take you to the second location." In this case the second location might have been in the attic, but it counted. And I was not going anywhere with a man I was certain was a murderer.

"Let me go," I repeated. "Or I'll start screaming."

"No you won't," Jordan said, reaching for my mouth with an open palm.

This guy doesn't know who he's messing with.

I was a city girl. This kind of manhandling warranted a broken nose.

I balled up my fist and uppercut him with my free hand. His head snapped back and his grip on my arm released. The minute he looked down at me again, his eyes hazy from the hit to his jaw, I snapped my second fist out and hit him right on the nose.

Jordan yelped and covered his face.

"Jerk," I yelled, as I descended the stairs two at a time. "Help!" I screamed it at the top of my lungs. "Help, help! I'm being attacked!"

Up and down the hall, doors opened, and members of the ballet company emerged, women and men, looking confused. Kate was among them. Cole was nowhere to be seen.

Oh no. I turned back looking up at Jordan on the stairs.

His top lip was bloody, his eyes watering.

There was a split second of silence, and then Jordan sprinted down the stairs. He blew past me, trying to get to the exit before anyone could stop him.

Thankfully, the male ballet dancers jumped to action and surrounded him. A tussle broke out, and there were shouts that drew more attention from other guests below. Beau appeared, yelling and telling everyone to calm down.

Once the metaphorical dust cleared, Jordan was on the floor, face down, with two ballet dancers holding him there.

"What in the name of—? What the heck is going on?" Beau thundered.

"He tried to attack me. Someone call 911 now." I had a terrible feeling in the pit of my stomach. I dropped my purse off my shoulder and onto the floor then ran for the attic stairs. I pulled myself up them.

The attic was perfectly neat.

Cole, the Ballet Master, was tied up in the corner, his head lolling to the right, and his eyes shut.

"Quick!" I screamed. "Call for an ambulance. Cole is up here. He needs medical attention." I ran to his side and dropped to my knees, hastily pressing two fingers to his throat and feeling for a pulse.

He groaned under his breath.

"He's alive," I yelled.

I wasn't sure if anyone had heard me, but there were shouts from downstairs, the thundering of footsteps as people came up to look.

Cole's chest rose and fell steadily, but he wasn't rousing, and I was pretty sure I knew why. Several round green tablets lay on the dresser next to the bed, and a few of them had been crushed. He'd forced them down Cole's throat.

He had the meds. Emma's oxycodone.

What felt like an eternity later, shouts rang out from below. The stern calls of cops.

Shawn appeared next to me. "Gina, it's OK. Stand back. The EMTs are here. They'll take care of them." He helped me up, walking me backward.

Several EMTs rushed in to take care of Cole, and my throat clogged with emotion as they worked to untie him and save his life.

"It's oxycodone poisoning," I called, shakily, pointing toward the pills on the dresser. "He was feeding him oxycodone. Jordan did it. Jordan had Emma's meds." Now that it was over, I couldn't stop shaking.

Shawn brought me to a chair in the corner of the room and sat me down. He kneeled beside me, his hand on my forearm. "It's OK, Gina. You're good. You done good."

I didn't know what to say. Tears stung the corners of my eyes as they removed Cole from the room.

"Did you get him?" I asked. "Did you arrest Jordan?"

"We've got him," Shawn said. "He's going to be charged with murder in the first degree."

"But Emma gave him the pills, didn't she? Didn't she? She has to be charged too."

"Emma gave him the pills," Shawn confirmed. "Gave Kate the pills to give to him, though Kate didn't know what they were. Jordan removed the pills from Kate's purse."

So, I'd been right. My assumption had been right. Strangely, I didn't care that much at the moment. All I really wanted was for Cole to be OK. If Jordan managed to kill his intended target after all of this, then...

It had been for nothing. And two innocents would have died because of Emma and Jordan's sick obsession with getting even.

Jordan had been so in love with Emma, he'd decided he'd go to the ends of the earth for her, even if that meant killing Cole and his own sister, mistake or not. It made me shaky and sick.

My breathing slowed and, once I was calm enough, we left the attic room and proceeded downstairs. The news came that Cole was stable, and relief shuddered through me.

It was over. The perpetrators had been caught, and Cole would survive.

"I owe you an apology," Shawn said. "I shouldn't have come down on you so hard about the video. Without your help, we wouldn't have solved this case. We had some evidence, we had Emma as a suspect, but you helped things fall into place. Thank you, Gina."

There were others in the hallway, and a few of the ballet dancers heard and gave a smattering of applause.

I smiled at them and at Shawn. "I'm just glad it's over," I said. "Things can get back to normal now."

As normal as they could be in Lake Basil.

Twenty-Six

Two weeks later...

ROMANO'S FAMILY RESTAURANT bustled with activity. Evening had fallen, and the tables were full of tourists and local Lake Basilites alike, all enjoying plates of pasta, slices of pizza, garlic bread, and refreshing drinks.

I stayed on the floor, watching my servers navigate the crowd. I would need another server soon—I'd already hired a bartender to take care of drinks orders, and the kitchen ran smoothly now that it was back in order.

Thankfully, the restaurant was a hit rather than a pariah after the events earlier in the month.

Uncle Rocco and Aunt Sofia had taken a table closest to the bar and were enjoying a romantic dinner, both of them with eyes glistening at how much of a success the restaurant had become. Matilda had popped by earlier in the night to get a takeout order of ravioli.

Violet approached the bar, and my heart turned over.

A complaint?

"Gina, that table over there wanted to talk to you about the cannelloni," she said. "Don't worry, I don't think it's a complaint."

I was still nervous as I walked up to the group of smiling customers.

A woman, a tourist was my guess as I didn't recognize her, waved me over.

"Are you the owner?" she asked.

"I am," I said. "Is there something I can help you with, ma'am?"

"I just wanted to compliment you on this fantastic cannelloni," she said, fluffing her dark hair. "It's fantastic!"

"Awesome. That is great to hear," I said. "I'll be sure to give your compliments to the chef."

"Please do," she said, then fluttered her eyelashes. She was pretty, young, definitely New York-Italian. Her lips were red as a rose, and she'd drawn on cat-eye eyeliner. She purred out the next words. "Is he the handsome guy I saw come out here just now?"

"Yes, ma'am," I replied.

"Then maybe I should give him my compliments in person." She laughed.

An older woman across the table snorted. "Lucia, behave, will you? You're embarrassing the rest of us who have to sit through your second-hand flirting."

"Relax, ma, I'm just playing." Lucia fluttered her lashes again. "What did you say your name was?" She directed that at me.

"Gina," I said. "I'm the owner of this establishment."

"Well, Gina, do you think you could ask that chef of yours if I can give him my number?" Lucia grabbed a napkin and scribbled down her name and number on it. Lucia Moretti.

She held out the napkin to me, wrist bent, as if she was asking me to kiss her ring rather than take an item from her.

"I'd love to, ma'am, but that wouldn't be appropriate," I said. "I do appreciate the compliments though, and I'll be sure to give them to the chef."

"Not appropriate?" Lucia arched a black, penciled eyebrow. "What are you, some kind of prude or somethin'?"

"No," I said. "Just the chef's girlfriend." The words came out louder than I'd intended and traveled through the restaurant.

Nearby, Violet hid a grin with such great effort that the corners of her lips tipped upward.

"Oh," Lucia said, shrugging. "Never stopped me before." Shameless.

"Have a lovely evening, folks," I said, and walked away from the table before I caused a scene.

The last thing I wanted was to break with professionalism. But I'd already done that. I'd gone back on what I'd said before our soft launch. I'd basically told this woman to back off my boyfriend, even though he was also my employee.

I rolled my eyes at myself for worrying about it.

I'd made my choice.

I pushed the kitchen door open and spotted Jacob behind the stove. "You good, Gina?"

"Yeah," I called back, in front of the chefs. "Just a lady outside wanted to give you her compliments on the cannelloni."

"That's great."

"And she wanted to give you her number," I said.

Jacob pulled a face. "Pass."

"Yeah, I told her I'm your girlfriend so she can't do that."

The other chefs exchanged glances with each other.

Jacob grinned broadly. "Oh yeah?"

"Yeah," I said. "She said it doesn't matter to her, but I figured I would just not give you the number, you know, since I'm in love with you and all."

One of the chefs dropped a spatula and cursed under his breath.

Jacob's grin grew even wider. "I love you too, Gina," he said. "But I gotta get back to work."

I laughed so loudly another chef jumped out of shock. "I'll leave you to it." I winked at him and left the kitchen, shaking my head at myself.

It felt like a little of that tension that I held constant had dissipated. The truth was, I didn't have to worry about Jacob being too good for me, or even too good to be true, because I deserved this. I deserved to be happy.

It had taken me so long to realize that, and now that I had, it was a weight off my shoulders.

I returned to the hostess station, my cheeks pink with joy, the restaurant full of the sounds of good memories in the making. New memories that would involve my family, my friends, and my future with the man I loved.

Join Gina, Matilda, Jumbo, and the gang as they investigate more murders in Lake Basil in the Ravioli Rub Out.

Craving More Cozy Mystery?

If you had fun with Ruby and Bee, you'll, love getting to know Charlie Mission and her butt-kicking grandmother, Georgina. You can read the first chapter of Charlie's story, *The Case of the Waffling Warrants*, below!

"Come in, Big G, come in." I spoke under my breath so that the flesh-colored microphone seated against my throat picked up my voice. "What is your status?"

My grandmother, Georgina—pet name Gamma, code name Big G—was out on a special operation. Reconnaissance at the newest guesthouse in our town, Gossip. The reason? First, she was an ex-spy, as was I, and second, the woman who'd opened the guesthouse was her mortal enemy and in direct competition with my grandmother's establishment, the Gossip Inn.

Who was this enemy, this bringer of potential financial doom?

A middle-aged woman with a penchant for wearing pashminas and annoying anyone who looked her way.

Jessie Belle-Blue.

It was rumored that even thinking the woman's name summoned a murder of crows.

"I repeat, Big G, what is your status?"

"I'm en route to the nest," my grandmother replied in my earpiece.

I let out a relieved sigh and exited my bedroom, heading downstairs to help with the breakfast service.

In the nine months since I had retired as a spy, life in Gossip had been normal. In the Gossip sense of the term. I'd expected that my job as a server, maid, and assistant would bring the usual level of "cat herding" inherent when working at the inn. Whether that involved tracking down runaway cats, literally, or providing a guest with a moist towelette after a fainting spell—tempers ran high in Gossip.

What was the reason for the craziness? Shoot, it had to be something in the water.

I took the main stairs two at a time and found my friend, the inn's chef, paging through her recipe book in the lime green kitchen. Lauren Harris wore her red hair in a French braid today, apron stretched over her pregnant belly.

"Morning," I said, "how are you today?"

"Madder than a fat cat on a diet." She slapped her recipe book closed and turned to me.

Uh oh. Looks like it's time for more cat herding.

"What's wrong?"

"My supplier is out of flour and sugar. Can you believe that?" Lauren huffed, smoothing her hands over her belly while the clock on the wall ticked away. Breakfast was in two hours and Lauren loved baking cupcakes as part of the meal.

"Do you have enough supplies to make cupcakes for this morning?"

"Yes. But just for today," Lauren replied. "The guests are going to love my new waffle cupcakes, and they'll be sore they can't get anymore after this batch is done. Why, I should go down there and wring Billy's neck for doing this to me. He knows I take an order of sugar and flour every week, and I get it at just above cost too. What's Georgina going to say?"

"Don't stress, Lauren," I said. "We'll figure it out."

"Right." She brightened a little. "I nearly forgot you're the one who "fixes" things around here." Lauren winked at me.

She was the only person in the entire town who knew that my grandmother and I had once been spies for the NSIB—the National Security Investigative Bureau. But the news that I had helped solve several murders had spread through town, and now, anybody and everybody with a problem would call me up asking for help. A lot of them offered me money. And I was selective about who I chose to help.

"I'll check it out for you if you'd like," I said. "The flour issue."

"Nah, that's OK. I'm sure Billy will get more stock this week. I'll lean on him until he squeals."

"Sounds like you've been picking up tips from Georgina."

Lauren giggled then returned to her super-secret recipe book—no one but she was allowed to touch it.

"What's on the menu this morning?" I asked.

Lauren was the boss in the kitchen—she told me what to do, and I followed her instructions precisely. If I did anything else, like trying to read the recipe for instance, the food would end up burned, missing ingredients or worse.

The only place I wasn't a "fixer" was in the Gossip Inn's kitchen.

"Bacon and eggs over easy, biscuits and gravy, waffle cupcakes and... oh, I can't make fresh baked bread, can I?"

"Tell her I'll bring some back with me from the

bakery." Gamma's voice startled me. Goodness, I'd forgotten about the earpiece—she could hear everything happening in the kitchen.

"I'll text Georgina and ask her to bring bread from the bakery."

"You're a lifesaver, Charlotte."

We set to work on the breakfast—it was 7:00 a.m. and we needed everything done within two hours—and fell into our easy rhythm of baking and cooking.

My grandmother entered the kitchen at around 8:30 a.m., dressed in a neat silk blouse and a pair of slacks rather than the black outfit she'd left in for her spy mission. Tall, willowy, and with neatly styled gray hair, Gamma had always reminded me of Helen Mirren playing the Queen.

"Good morning, ladies," she said, in her prim, British accent. "I bring bread and tidings."

"What did you find out?" I asked.

"No evidence of the supposed ghost tours," Gamma said.

We'd started hosting ghost tours at the inn recently, so of course Jessie Belle-Blue wanted to do the same. She was all about under-cutting us, but, thankfully, the Gossip Inn had a legacy and over 1,000 positive reviews on TripAdvisor.

Breakfast time arrived, and the guests filled the quaint dining area with its glossy tables, creaking wooden floors, and egg yolk yellow walls. Chatter and laughter leaked through the swinging kitchen doors with their porthole windows.

"That's my cue," I said, dusting off my apron, and heading out into the dining room.

I picked up a pot of coffee from the sideboard where we kept the drinks station and started my rounds.

Most of the guests had gathered around a center table in the dining room, and bursts of laughter came from the group, accompanied by the occasional shout.

I elbowed my way past a couple of guests—nobody could accuse me of having great people skills—apologizing along the way until I reached the table. The last time something like this had happened, a murder had followed shortly afterward.

Not this time. No way.

"—the last thing she'd ever hear!" The woman seated at the table, drawing the attention, was vaguely familiar. She wore her dark hair in luscious curls, and tossed it as she spoke, looking down her upturned nose at the people around the table.

"What happened then, Mandy?" Another woman asked, her hands clasped together in front of her stomach.

Mandy? Wait a second, isn't this Mandy Gilmore?

Gamma had mentioned her once before—Mandy was

a massive gossip in town. Why wasn't she staying at her house?

"What happened? Well, she ran off with her tail between her legs, of course. She'll soon learn not to cross me. Heaven knows, I always repay my debts."

"What, like a Lannister from *Game of Thrones*?" That had come from a taller woman with ginger curls.

"Shut up, Opal," Mandy replied. "You have no idea what we're talking about, and even if you did, you wouldn't have the intelligence to comprehend it."

The crowd let out various 'oofs' in response to that. The woman next to me clapped her hand over her mouth.

"You're all talk, Gilmore." Opal lifted a hand and yammered it at the other woman. "You act like you're a threat, but we know the truth around here."

"The truth?" Mandy leaned in, pressing her hands flat onto the tabletop, the crystal vase in the center rattling. "And what's that, Opal, darling? I'd love to hear it."

"That you're a failure. You sold your house, left Gossip with your head in the clouds, told everyone you were going to become a successful businesswoman, and now you're back. Back to scrape together the pieces of the life you have left."

"Witch!" Mandy scraped her chair back.

"All right, all right," I said, setting down the coffee pot

on the table. "That's enough, ladies. Everyone head back to their tables before things get out of hand."

Both Opal and Mandy stared daggers at me.

I flashed them both smiles. "We wouldn't want to ruin breakfast, would we? Lauren's prepared waffle cupcakes."

That distracted them. "Waffle cupcakes?" Opal's brow wrinkled. "How's that going to work?"

"Let's talk about it at your table." I grabbed my coffee pot and walked her away from Mandy. The crowd slowly dispersed, people muttering regret at having missed out on a show. The Gossip Inn was popular for its constant conflict.

If the rumors didn't start here then they weren't worth repeating. That was the mantra, anyway.

I seated Opal at her table, and she pursed her lips at me. "You shouldn't have interrupted. That woman needs a piece of my mind."

"We prefer peace of mind at the inn." I put up another of my best smiles.

Compared to what I'd been through in the past—hiding out from my rogue spy ex-husband and eventually helping put him behind bars when he found me—dealing with the guests was a cakewalk.

"What brings you to Gossip, Opal?" I asked.

"I live here," she replied, waspishly. "I'm staying here while they're fumigating my house. Roaches."

"Ah." I struggled not to grimace. Thankfully, my cell phone buzzed in the front pocket of my apron and distracted me. "Coffee?"

"I don't take caffeine." And she said it like I'd offered her an illegal substance too.

"Call me if you need anything." I hurried off before she could make good on that promise, bringing my phone out of my pocket.

I left the coffee pot on the sideboard, moving into the Gossip Inn's spacious foyer, the chandelier overhead off, but catching light in glimmers. The tables lining the hall were filled with trinkets from the days when the inn had been a museum—an eclectic collection of bits and bobs.

"This is Charlotte Smith," I answered the call—I would never get to use my true last name, Mission, again, but it was safer this way.

"Hello, Charlotte." A soft, rasping voice. "I've been trying to get through to you. I'm desperate."

"Who is this?"

"My name is Tina Rogers, and I need your help."

"My help."

"Yes," she said. "I understand that you have a certain set of skills. That you fix people's problems?"

"I do. But it depends on the problem and the price." I didn't have a set fee for helping people, but if it drew me away from the inn for long, I had to charge. I was technically a consultant now. Sort of like a P.I. without the fedora and coffee-stained shirt.

"My mother will handle your fee," Tina said. "I've asked her to text you about it, but I... I don't have long to talk. They're going to pull me off the phone soon."

"Who?"

"The police," she replied. "I'm calling you from the holding cell at the Gossip Police Station. I've been arrested on false charges, and I need you to help me prove my innocence."

"Miss Rogers, it's probably a better idea to invest in a lawyer." But I was tempted. It had been a long time since I'd felt useful.

"No! I'm not going to a lawyer. I'm going to make these idiots pay for ever having arrested me."

I took a breath. "OK. Before I accept your... case, I'll need to know what happened. You'll need to tell me everything." I glanced through the open doorway that led into the dining room. No one looked unhappy about the lack of service yet.

"I can't tell you everything now. I don't have much time."

"So give me the *CliffsNotes*."

"I was arrested for breaking into and vandalizing Josie Carlson's bakery, The Little Cake Shop. Apparently, they found my glove there—it was specially embroidered, you see—but it's not mine because—" The line went dead.

"Hello? Miss Rogers?" I pulled the cellphone away from my ear and frowned at the screen. "Darn."

My interest was piqued. A mystery case about a break-in that involved the local bakery? Which just so happened to be run by one of my least favorite people in Gossip?

And when I'd just started getting bored with the push and pull of everyday life at the inn?

Count me in.

Want to read more? You can grab **the first book** in *the Gossip Cozy Mystery series* on all major retailers.

Happy reading, friend!

Paperbacks Available by Rosie A. Point

A Burger Bar Mystery series

The Fiesta Burger Murder

The Double Cheese Burger Murder

The Chicken Burger Murder

The Breakfast Burger Murder

The Salmon Burger Murder

The Cheesy Steak Burger Murder

A Bite-sized Bakery Cozy Mystery series

Murder by Chocolate

Marzipan and Murder

Creepy Cake Murder

Murder and Meringue Cake

Murder Under the Mistletoe

Murder Glazed Donuts

Choc Chip Murder

Macarons and Murder

Candy Cake Murder

Murder by Rainbow Cake

Murder With Sprinkles

Trick or Murder

Christmas Cake Murder

S'more Murder

Murder and Marshmallows

Donut Murder

Buttercream Murder

Chocolate Cherry Murder

Caramel Apple Murder

Red, White 'n Blue Murder

Pink Sprinkled Murder

Murder by Milkshake

Murder by Cupid Cake

Caramel Cupcake Murder

Cake Pops and Murder

A Milly Pepper Mystery series

Maple Drizzle Murder

A Sunny Side Up Cozy Mystery series

Murder Over Easy

Muffin But Murder

Chicken Murder Soup

Murderoni and Cheese

Lemon Murder Pie

A Gossip Cozy Mystery series

The Case of the Waffling Warrants

The Case of the Key Lime Crimes

The Case of the Custard Conspiracy

A Mission Inn-possible Cozy Mystery series

Vanilla Vendetta

Strawberry Sin

Cocoa Conviction

Mint Murder

Raspberry Revenge

Chocolate Chills

A Very Murder Christmas series

Dachshund Through the Snow

Owl Be Home for Christmas

Made in the USA
Monee, IL
04 June 2025

18774524R00111